" . . .fast-moving, entertaining stories."
—Bill Crider, *The Gold Medal Corner*

"Marvin Albert was the real deal . . ."
—*Paperback Warrior*

"The action is swift, the writing is solid, and the plotting is a step above the usual . . . *The Girl With No Place to Hide* is the strongest of the Jake Barrow books."
—George Kelley, *Murder Off the Rack*

THE GIRL WITH NO PLACE TO HIDE

Marvin Albert
writing as Nick Quarry

Black Gat Books

Black Gat Books • Eureka California

THE GIRL WITH NO PLACE TO HIDE

Published by Black Gat Books
A division of Stark House Press
1315 H Street
Eureka, CA 95501, USA
griffinskye3@sbcglobal.net
www.starkhousepress.com

THE GIRL WITH NO PLACE TO HIDE
Originally published by Gold Medal Books, Greenwich, as by Nick
Quarry, and copyright © 1959 by Nick Quarry.

ISBN-13: 978-1-951473-49-5

Cover and text design by ¡caliente!design, Austin, Texas
Proofreading by Bill Kelly
Cover art by Ed Balcourt

First Stark House Press/Black Gat Edition: October 2021

ONE

She came slowly, hesitantly through the bead curtains at one end of the small room, a slender, lovely, olive-skinned girl wearing transparent black harem pants that covered nothing but her legs. The rest of her was naked. From behind the curtain the sound of a muted instrument began an eerie wailing, punctuated by the dull, steady thump of a soft-skinned drum. The small room was lighted only by the dim reddish spotlight that followed her sinuous movements.

Her dance began slowly, gathering steam relentlessly. For a long moment she just stood there swaying, leaning slightly forward, staring wide-eyed into the darkness concealing the small all-male audience. Her breasts rose and fell with each breath that hissed through her bared white teeth. She glanced back over her shoulder with pretended terror, as though someone were pursuing her.

Then the drum beat louder, monotonously, excitingly, and the olive-skinned girl moved sensually to it, dancing with a control of her body that revealed ballet training. Her bare feet slithered over the floor, her arms raised as though warding off a blow, her face held its look of fright. She twisted and writhed to the wail of the eerie instrument, her small hands clutching with pretended pain at a different part of her each time the drum thudded, as though an invisible whip was flicking her. Caught in the grip of the insistent music, she cringed, whirled, stomped, trembled, cowered. Her hands clutched at her tiny waist, her buttocks, her breasts, her thighs. . . .

It was a hot night out, and I'd dropped into the Oran Club as much for the air conditioning as for a cold beer. But the girl's dance seemed to have stopped the air conditioning completely.

The Oran was a Greenwich Village trap, and she'd

been dancing in the main room out front for the past month. But not like this. I'd seen her act a couple times, out front. But this was the back room. The performance she was putting on now would have gotten the place closed, if she'd tried it out front.

I felt my breathing quicken as I watched her twisting through her dance of torment. Finally she sank to her knees, her head hanging forward, her breasts shaking, her shoulders heaving to the wail and thud that pounded louder, louder . . . Still on her knees, she let her torso slowly sink back, swaying and writhing, till her hair touched the floor behind her. Her legs straightened, her arms stretched out, till she lay spread-eagled on the floor. The eerie music stopped abruptly. She lay quiet, panting, staring up at some unseen thing above her. And then the reddish spotlight playing over her nudity flickered out, plunging the room into total darkness.

When the wall lamps snapped on, she was gone.

I turned my head and looked at Steve Canby sitting beside me. Canby was a fight manager who also owned a piece of the Oran Club. He was a middle-aged, medium-sized man with a sharp-featured, worried face, thinning gray hair and too much weight around the middle. At the moment a grin was fighting the perpetual worry of his face, and beads of sweat dotted his forehead and cheeks. I got out my handkerchief and mopped my own face.

"That," Canby whispered huskily, "is how Cecile's gonna perform down in Havana. Something, ain't it?"

I nodded agreement. "Something, all right." I washed the rest of my beer down my parched throat. "It's been a privilege, Steve."

It had been. I'd known Canby fairly well for a long time, had done him some favors, and we liked each other. Which was why he'd invited me to the back room to watch Cecile show a small, select group of customers how different her act was going to be in Havana.

"I hear," I mentioned, "that you and Cecile've been seeing a lot of each other the past month."

"Yeah," Canby said fervently. "What a doll. . . . Shame this's her last night in New York."

"Good thing," I told him. "You should be keeping your mind on the fight Friday night."

The best of the bruisers in Canby's stable, a fast, bright Negro kid named Frankie Sims, was scheduled to fight Rocky Gabe at the Garden Friday night. The winner would get a go at the middleweight champ.

"Nothing to worry about," Canby said. "The fight's in the bag for my boy."

"Rocky Gabe hits like a truck."

"Sure. But Franklie'll out-dance him, out-box him, and cut him to ribbons. You can bet on it."

"I might. That's why I want your mind on the fight, instead of sexy Cecile."

"Jealous, jealous."

I grinned and nodded. "That's a fact."

He glanced toward the bead curtains through which Cecile had vanished. "I got a date with her, soon as she gets dressed. We're going to a party uptown . . . Whyn't you come along with us?"

I considered it, shook my head. "It's the end of a long, hard day for me, Steve. Besides, if you've got Cecile all sewed up, there's no incentive for me to go."

Canby laughed at my open envy, slapped my shoulder and stood up. "Okay, Jake. Be seeing you around."

He headed for the bead curtains. I got up and walked out of the back room and into the front part of the Oran Club. There were a lot of empty leather-padded stools in front of the bar, this close to closing time. I perched on one of them, ordered another tall cold beer. The air conditioning seemed to be working better out there.

I was nibbling my third beer, taking my time with

it, when a tall, strongly built girl wearing satin slacks and a knit sweater, both in the same pale blue, hurried in through the entrance door. She halted just inside and looked around anxiously, giving me time for a good stare.

Her features weren't regular enough for her to be called beautiful. Her mouth was a bit too wide, her nose a bit too thick. But she had a pair of saucy, snapping dark eyes, and a mass of black hair soft and smooth as down. She had a downright arrogant figure, too. And a way of holding it without thinking about it calculated to make a man squirm.

When she didn't see whatever she was looking for, she hurried to the bar a few stools down from me and asked the bartender quickly: "Is Steve Canby around?"

"He was," the bartender told her. "I'll take a look."

He walked down the back of the bar and through the door into the back room. The girl in the blue sweater and slacks perched one buttock on the edge of a stool and gnawed at her full lower lip. I observed her with pleasure and interest. She caught me watching her, and a look of fright came over her sultry face. It reminded me of the way Cecile had looked over her shoulder during the dance in the back room. Only this girl wasn't pretending.

It made me feel like the monster from the black lagoon. I turned my head away and made a point of not ogling her any more. But when I looked in the mirror behind the bar, I saw her glance my way. And she still looked afraid of me.

The bartender came back behind the bar, shaking his head at her. "Left five minutes ago."

She stared at him, looking lost, helpless. "Where'd Steve go? Do you know?"

"Uh-uh. Some party uptown is all I know."

"You don't know where?"

"Nope."

She gnawed her lip some more, staring at him worriedly. Then she muttered, "Gimme a Scotch. Make it a double."

"With what?"

"Nothing. Straight."

He poured the double Scotch into a glass and she poured it down her throat, shuddering but not putting the glass down till she'd finished all of it. She slapped a bill and some change on the bar and hurried out.

A few minutes later I finished my beer, decided I'd had enough. I paid the tab and sauntered out into the dark, hot night.

My Chevy was parked at the curb a few doors down from the Oran Club. I got in, started the motor and switched on the headlights. It was after two-thirty A.M. by then, and the street and sidewalks were getting that deserted look. I pulled the Chevy away from the curb, drove to the end of the block, and turned into the dark, narrow cross street, heading in the direction of my apartment.

My headlights caught the girl in the blue slacks and sweater. She was up ahead, on the pavement to my right, struggling frantically with a big, bulky man who towered over her. I got only a split-second glimpse of the two of them, before the man yanked her out of the headlights, into the darkness of the alley behind him.

It took me another split second to bring the Chevy to a jolting halt and leap out onto the pavement. I sprinted for the alley, wishing I had a gun on me. But the surprise of my sudden appearance helped somewhat.

She was down on her knees before him. He was bent over her, his hands around her throat. I couldn't see either of them distinctly, but in that narrow, shadowed alley he looked big enough to take on a hippo with a fly-swatter. He let her go and straightened as I swerved into the alley with them. His hand flashed under his jacket and came out with an automatic. But by then I was close enough. I kicked as though I were trying to send a football the whole hundred yards.

The hard toe of my shoe struck his forearm, knocking it upwards, sending the gun flying out of his hand into the darkness. He gasped with the pain of it, then came at me, arms wide and reaching. I set myself and hit him flush on the chin with my right fist, getting everything I had behind it. It was a mistake. It was like hitting a boulder. My hand felt broken. He let out a grunt and fell back against the wall of the alley, but he didn't go down. He shook his head, shoved off the wall, and swung a fist at my face. It went past my ear like a freight train.

In dodging it, I tripped over the girl's legs. Before I could catch my balance, he had me by the throat with both massive-fingered hands, squeezing. His hands cut off my blood and air instantly. My vision blurred. I flailed out at him blindly. I hit him, too. But it didn't mean anything to him.

The hands around my throat tightened, lifting me till my feet were hanging off the ground. My brain swelled in the confines of my skull, pushed against the back of my eyes. Bloodshot blackness swirled before my face. I kicked him in the shinbone, as hard as I could. His hold around my neck loosened. I kneed him in the groin. He let out a sob of agony and dropped me, bending over his pain.

I landed on my feet, jerked up a leg, brought my heel down across the top of his instep. He gasped again, torso bending lower. I yanked my knee up sharply into his face, felt the bone of his nose go. He stumbled backwards, arms flung wide, a perfect target. This time I didn't waste it trying to break my hands on him. I kicked him in the stomach with all I had. He made a horrible belching sound, and slowly settled to the cement floor of the alley. When he was all the way down in a motionless, hard-breathing knot, I straightened and turned my head back and forth a couple times, till my neck felt attached to my spine once more.

Then I looked at the girl. She was rising to her feet, rubbing her throat with her hands. I rubbed my own throat. "Me, too. You all right?"

She nodded. In the shadows, her face was still twisted with terror. But she wasn't afraid of me anymore. "I . . . I thought you were one of them," she whispered raggedly. "Thank God you weren't."

I wandered down the alley, looking till I found his automatic. "I'll stay here with him," I told her. "You get to the nearest phone and call the cops."

She stared at me for a moment as though she hadn't heard me. But she had. "No . . . No cops . . . Please! . . . It's not something for the cops." She came closer, grabbing my arm and clinging.

"Please," she begged. "I just want to get away from here, quickly . . . Just take me away. Please!"

It was her business. For all I knew, the unconscious bruiser might be her husband. I didn't think so. But it was still her business. I removed the clip from the automatic, tossed it far down the alley, dropped the gun on the guy's bulky, still figure. Then I took the girl out of the alley, to my car.

I helped her into the front seat, went around and climbed in behind the steering wheel. She was huddled against the car door, breathing hard, her hands still to her throat, her smooth mass of raven hair hanging disordered around her face.

"Where to?"

She thought about it, shook her head. "I don't know. Just drive, any place. Hurry."

I got the car in gear, let out the brake and drove away. As we reached the end of the block I looked up in the rear-view mirror. The big guy I'd tangled with came staggering out of the alley back there. He reached

the curb and stood there, bent over and swaying, gazing after my Chevy.

I took the next corner, turned several more in
reaching Fourteenth Street, checking the rear-view a
couple times more to make sure no other car was tail-
ing mine.

She hadn't said anything more, so finally I asked it.
"What's it all about?"

It blurted out of her, almost hysterically. "They got
Ernie . . . now they're after me. It . . ."

She shut it off abruptly, as though she'd suddenly
realized she was saying it loud enough for me to hear.

I headed west on Fourteenth. "If you're in some
kind of trouble," I told her, "I just might be able to
help. That's my job."

She looked at me then, her snapping dark eyes big
and puzzled. "What's that mean?"

"I'm a private detective."

"Oh?" It interested her. She thought about it.
"What's your name?"

"Jake Barrow."

"I never heard of you."

"You've got a lot of company. But I still might be
able to help. If you want to talk to me about it."

She shook her head, making it pretty definite. "Got
a cigarette on you?"

I handed her the pack. She lit one, puffed at it
fiercely for a few seconds, then leaned back in the seat.

We reached the Hudson River docks, cut onto the
wide, cobbled street under the elevated West Side
Highway where the smell of truck exhaust fumes
clashed with the odors of dead fish and rotting dock
pilings. That was one place in town that kept busy
through the dark hours. Trucks jammed the street
along the docks, tangling as they came in, got loaded,
fought their way out again, each truck a slowly moving
piece in a massively intricate jigsaw puzzle. I got the

Chevy through the tangle to the Battery, made the swing around the bottom tip of Manhattan and cruised up the Franklin D. Roosevelt Drive, where the highway lights gleamed on the oily dark water of the East River to my right.

Beside me, the girl had finished her cigarette without volunteering any more information. She tossed the butt out the open side window and said, "God, I need a drink bad."

"Sure . . . You got a name, by the way?"

"Angela." She didn't mention any last name.

"I know a couple places where we could still get a drink," I told her.

She shook her head, her face getting a tight look again. "No. I don't want to go to another bar and maybe get spotted again."

I turned left off the Drive, back onto Fourteenth. I checked the rear-view mirror again as I did it. She had me that nervous. No other car turned off the Drive behind us.

"Where do you live?" she asked me quietly.

"Not far. In the Village."

"Got any liquor there?"

"Uh-huh. Be my guest?"

"I'd love to," she murmured, and reached out to squeeze my arm, hard.

She'd love to. I believed her. She was more than willing to go up to my place. She was desperately eager.

The tension of her made me look in the rear-view mirror one last time. There was still no one following us. But I couldn't say, afterward, that I'd had no warning I was getting into something messy.

TWO

My apartment was on the second floor of a four-storey building, directly over the downstairs diner. It consisted of a pretty big living room, a tiny kitchenette, a smallish bedroom and a bathroom. The furniture had been second-hand when Hoover was a boy, but it was clean and comfortable. I turned on a couple lamps and closed the blinds. She sat on the sofa and kicked off her shoes while I went into the kitchenette and mixed a couple stiff drinks.

When I came back into the living room with the drinks, Angela had her bare feet tucked up under her on the sofa and was looking content as a cat accepting a new home. Being safe inside seemed to have drained the fear out of her. She had a look on her face that matched her figure now; an arrogant sureness of her female impact on men. Me, at the moment.

I sat on the sofa with her and we drank. We talked a bit, too. But not about her. She was curious about me. I told her the things she wanted to know, mostly about the kind of work I did. And all the while she studied me as though she were sizing me up for something.

We were on our third drink before I got anything out of her. It wasn't much.

"You were looking for Steve Canby back there at the Oran," I said. "Known Canby long?"

"A while," she told me, guardedly. "Do you know Steve?"

"We've had some laughs together. Think his boy, Frankie Sims, is going to win Friday?"

She shrugged, uninterested in the subject. "I wouldn't know about that." She eyed me cautiously, and I had the feeling she was about to confide something in me. I was wrong. After a while she finished off her third drink, gulping it down.

I tried again. "Where do you live?"

She looked down at the empty glass, rolling it slowly between her palms, considering my question.

Finally, she said, "No place. At the moment." She

didn't try very hard to make it believable. She looked up, meeting my eyes. I decided that her dark eyes were actually black as her hair. She didn't have to be beautiful; everything about her was provocative. And no one knew it better than she did.

She smiled at the way I was looking at her, the corners of her lips quirking up. "I'm from out of town," she drawled softly. Her smile drifted away and she added, "And I'm heading back as soon as I can."

"What's stopping you?"

"Money. I need some dough to get out of New York and stay out for a long time. . . . Meanwhile, I've got to hole up somewhere, stay out of sight."

"You could still tell me your troubles," I suggested.

Angela shook her head. "You couldn't help."

She studied me, her dark eyes speculating and wise—the eyes of a woman who'd known an awful lot of men, awfully well. She watched me finish my drink, and asked, "Another?" When I nodded, she murmured, "Let me." She took my glass and hers, got up and headed for the kitchen. She walked with arrogant femaleness.

When she came back with the drinks, I saw by her face that she'd made up her mind about my usefulness to her. Then I saw she'd opened all the buttons down the front of her sweater. She wasn't wearing a bra. She sat down beside me and leaned slightly to hand me my drink.

"I've *got* to find some place to hole up for a while," she repeated with soft insistence.

"I could take you to a hotel," I suggested.

She shook her head. "I don't want to go out again tonight." She drank from her glass. Her full lips glistened wetly with liquor. "Maybe it'd be smart for me not to go out anywhere again for a few days. Until . . ."

She didn't finish it. She looked at me with thoughtful confidence—confidence in her effect on me. Then she stood up and put her glass on the lamp table next to the sofa. "I feel safe here with you," she purred. "I'd like staying here with you for a few days."

She stood close, looking down at me. "You won't mind my being here," she promised. "Not at all." And her eyes promised more.

It added up to a flat offer: the use of her body for the use of my apartment.

"Well?" she murmured. "Do I stay?"

"Sure. But you don't have to pay for it."

She frowned. "What does that mean?"

"It means if you're afraid to go out, you're welcome to stay here a while. No charge."

"Oh . . ." She eyed me curiously, then shrugged a bit angrily. "Okay." She picked up her drink. "Well, thanks for the free room and board, mister." She sipped her drink, looking blank-faced at me.

"You're welcome," I growled. "And now will you for crissake kindly button your sweater?"

The corners of her mouth quirked again in that funny way. "I thought maybe I didn't affect you," she said.

"The hell you say."

"Oh?" She set the glass back down on the table. "Well, in that case . . ."

The phone rang.

I got off the sofa and went to it, glancing at my watch and frowning. I picked it up and said, "Yeah?" into it.

"Jake Barrow?" It was a woman's voice. A husky, deep-in-the-throat voice.

"Uh-huh."

"I need your help, Mr. Barrow."

"At three-thirty in the morning?" I asked, irritably.

"Yes . . . I'm sorry. It has to be now. I'll pay for your trouble. I need you at once."

"Who are you?"

"Mary Soames," she said through the phone. "Mrs.

Bertrand Soames." She said it as though it should mean something to me. It didn't.

"A friend of mine," she went on, "someone who knows you, gave me your number. He recommended you highly."

"Has he got a name?" I demanded.

"I can't talk about it over the phone," she said. "Please . . . I'll explain when you get here."

"Look, lady . . ." I started to say.

She interrupted me with three words: "Two hundred dollars."

I breathed for a while, savoring the sound of the money.

"For a couple hours' work," she added.

"What kind of work?"

"I'm paying a man for the return of some letters I wrote," the husky voice said in my ear. "I want you with me to make sure I get what I'm paying for. That's all. Please."

"Where do I come?"

She gave me the name and address of a hotel in the Bronx. "I'm in Room 6235. Will you come right away?"

"Are you registered under your own name?"

"Yes."

I asked her quickly, "What's your phone number there?"

She told it to me. I didn't detect any pause before she answered.

"Please hurry," she begged, and hung up.

I put down the phone slowly.

"What's up?" Angela murmured from the sofa behind me.

"Let you know in a minute," I told her. It could still be a gag. I looked up the Bronx hotel in the phone book. It was the number she'd given me.

I picked up the phone again and dialed the number. The answering voice on the hotel switchboard was a man's.

I asked to be put through to Room 6235.

There was a click in the connection, and Mary Soames' deep, husky voice came through: "Yes?"

"This is Barrow," I told her. "Just checking. I'm on my way."

I hung up again and turned to look at Angela. "Got to go out for a couple hours."

"Do you have to?"

"For two hundred bucks, I have to."

Money meant something to her, too. Out of the corner of my eye I saw her nod.

"All right," she said. "But don't be too long."

"Make yourself at home." I went into the bedroom, got the Magnum out of the drawer, slipped it into the shoulder harness and put the gun in its holster.

Most blackmailers don't play it that rough. Especially ones that work the love-letters-from-married-women gimmick. But you never can be sure.

Angela came into the bedroom as I got into my jacket. She stretched out on the bed. She still hadn't buttoned her sweater.

"I'll hurry back," I promised as I headed for the apartment door.

Her voice drifted out to me lazily: "I'll be waiting."

I made good time driving uptown through Manhattan toward the Bronx. There was no traffic other than an occasional cab or bus.

The hotel was a small, going-to-seed one just across the Harlem River. I got a crawly feeling down the small of my back as soon as I saw it. 6235 was too big a room number for a place that size.

The lobby was small, old-fashioned and homey. There was a plump-faced boy in his early twenties behind the short desk. His elbows leaned on the desk as he studied the college biology textbook before him. He was too absorbed in the book to hear me approach.

"Room 6235?" I asked him.

He looked up quickly, startled. I repeated the question.

He frowned and said, "What?" Then he remembered, and he got a frozen, unsure look.

"Is Mary Soames, or Mrs. Bertrand Soames, registered here?"

"I . . ." he cleared his throat uncertainly, glanced at the register. "I'll see."

He started to reach for the register.

"Don't bother," I told him. "Who's on the switchboard?"

His fingers writhed on the desk top. "I . . . I am, sir."

"I just called and asked for Room 6235. You put me through to Mrs. Soames."

He stared at me, licking his lips nervously. He was frightened, but not of anything more serious than losing his job.

"How much did she pay you?" I asked him gently.

The gentle approach didn't work. He licked his lips, looked down at the open textbook for a while, hunting an answer to my question there. The book was open to two full-page sketches of human skeletons. Even if they weren't the answers to my questions, they seemed to give him food for thought.

I unbuttoned the front of my jacket and hooked the thumb of my left hand on the side of my belt. This pulled my jacket open enough for the butt of the Magnum to show.

He looked up at me again at last, and saw the gun. The plump healthy flesh of his face sagged with shock. His eyes got a glazed-over look.

"Tell me about her," I said, not at all gently this time.

He opened his mouth three times before he managed to get the first words out. After that they came fast. He was eager to please.

"She came in about an hour ago. Gave me five bucks. She said if anybody called and asked for Room 6235, or for a Mrs. Soames, I was to put the call through to her on the house phone over there."

He jerked his head at a phone on the wall shelf next to the desk. His hands were clenched tightly together, their knuckles white.

"I . . . I'm real sorry if I . . . I can use the money and I didn't think there was anything wrong with . . . I thought it was some kind of joke."

"Some things aren't worth doing for five bucks, or a hundred. Tell me the rest of it."

I made sure the butt of the Magnum continued to show. He was fascinated by it.

"She made a call from the booth over there." He nodded at the pay phone booth in the far corner of the little lobby. "You phoned just as she was coming out of the booth. I put the call to the house phone and she took it. . . . I . . . Mister, I'm real sorry. Honest. I . . ."

"Do you know her? Her real name?"

"No I don't. Just Soames, like she said."

"Ever seen her before?"

"Never. She just walked in an hour ago and . . ."

"Describe her."

His Adam's apple jerked up and down. He wiped a weary hand across his face. But he couldn't take his eyes from the gun in my shoulder holster. "She . . . She was pretty tall. For a woman. Dark red hair. Kinda slinky figure, you know?"

"Young? Old?"

"Pretty young . . . I mean, she was older'n me, but young. Real good-looking, too."

"Dressed how?"

"I don't know. Something black. I didn't notice. Mister . . . Please . . . What's this all about?"

All I knew was that I'd been suckered. And I

thought I knew why.

I strode away from the badly frightened desk clerk to the corner booth, got in and dropped a dime in the coin slot, dialed my apartment.

By the third ring, I was sure of it. But I let the phone ring in my apartment four more times before I hung up and rushed back out to my car.

THREE

My door was unlocked. I knew damn well I'd locked it on my way out, less than an hour before.

I went in fast, with the Magnum ready in my fist, made a quick tour of the rooms. The apartment was empty. I'd half-expected to find Angela beaten or dead, so it was a relief that she was just gone. But not much of a relief. I was sure Angela had had no intention of leaving my place that night. She'd expected to stay and wait for my return. Something had changed her mind. Or somebody had changed it for her.

I pushed the Magnum's safety back on as I took another, slower, look around. There were no signs of a struggle. Everything was where I'd left it—except the pale blue sweater and Angela. They were gone.

Then I saw the small scrap of paper on the table beside the phone. It had been torn off the appointment pad there, and the pencil had been used to scribble something on it.

I picked up the scrap of paper and read what had been hastily scrawled on it: "Jake—I'll call you later. Angela." I dropped the note, lit a cigarette, and stood there a while smoking and trying to puzzle it out. There were a number of possible explanations, none of them worth anything as guesses. But she'd written that she'd call me later. Later was a loose term that might mean in an hour, or sometime tomorrow, or next week.

Finally I had a few shots of rye to calm myself

down, stripped, and went to bed. It wasn't easy, but I managed to beat the dawn in falling asleep.

It was almost eleven in the morning when I woke. I crawled out of bed and phoned my answering service. There were no calls for me at my office so far that morning. Not from Angela, not from my eager new client, not from anyone.

I phoned down to the diner and ordered myself a combination breakfast-lunch. I shaved, showered, dressed and ate the meal the boy from the diner brought up. By then it was noon, and Angela still hadn't called.

Reading the morning newspapers that the boy had brought up with my meal, I couldn't shake the edgy feeling that I ought to be doing something about Angela. According to the note she'd written me, she'd left under her own steam. But it didn't fit. I'd been suckered all the way up to the Bronx. It had to have something to do with Angela. Somebody had wanted her alone in the apartment. I'd fallen for the gag, so now I felt responsible.

I finished the *Times* and *Tribune*. There was a revolution in South America, a housing scandal in Brooklyn, another crisis in Berlin, renewed tension along the India-Pakistan border, and no call from Angela. I finished my second cup of coffee and picked up the *Daily News*.

There was a gory photo on the front page of a man with his wrists and ankles tied together behind his back, lying on a rug. He was wearing just his undershorts. There were dark bruises on his bare torso, arms and legs. His face was broken and bloodied beyond recognition. His skull had been caved in above his left ear.

The corpse had a good build; muscular, lean in the middle and hips, wide in the chest and shoulders. His chest was hairless. He lay on his right side on the rug.

The picture had been shot from above. The news photographer had probably stood on a chair to get all of the corpse into the shot, and used a flashbulb. It was a clear, sharp picture.

You could see the clenched fists below the twine that bit into wrists and ankles, binding them tightly together behind him. You could see the straining of the neck muscles that had turned his head so the face looked up at the camera. The strips of surgical tape over his mouth that had muffled his screams were still in place. There wasn't enough left of the rest of the face to make out what its expression had been, at the end.

His name was Ernest Lewis.

"They got Ernie . . . now they're after me."

Angela had said that last night, before she'd clammed up on me.

There were a lot of guys named Ernest in New York. Probably a coincidence.

There wasn't much of a news story with the picture. His name was Ernest Lewis and he had been a commercial photographer. He'd been found by a cop at about one-thirty that morning in his Greenwich Village apartment. The cop had been summoned by Lewis' downstairs neighbor, who had heard a woman scream in Lewis' apartment. The cop found the door of the apartment open, and Lewis dead like that on the floor. He'd been brutally beaten, then killed by a final crushing blow on the head with some blunt instrument. The woman who had screamed, whoever she was, was gone. At the time the *News* went to press with the picture, the police still had no notion who'd committed the murder, or why it had been done.

The *Daily Mirror* had it on its third page: a picture of the blanket-shrouded corpse being carried out of the building on a stretcher. The *Mirror's* short item on the murder carried only one extra bit of information: Ernest Lewis' address.

Ernie . . . Ernest Lewis. And a woman who had

screamed and then vanished. Angela?

The odds were still that it was a coincidence. But I didn't have any old business to work on at the moment. And another call to my answering service netted me no new business. It was past noon by then. Angela still hadn't phoned. I thought about her; and about the slinky redhead who'd lured me out of the apartment with the phony phone call. Then, too, there was the big hulk who'd tried to strangle Angela in the alley . . .

It was remembering him that made me strap on the loaded Magnum before slipping into my lightweight wash-and-wear jacket. He'd been pretty big, but the punch packed by a .357 Magnum was a lot bigger.

It was hot and muggy out. I'd have preferred doing without my jacket. But even in New York the sight of a guy walking around wearing a holstered gun in plain sight under his arm would have collected a crowd.

Ernest Lewis' address was below Washington Square, in one of those narrow cross streets sprinkled with Italian grocery stores and bars, avant-garde coffee houses, and cheap, underworld-owned nightclubs. It was a lean, four-storey red-brick house with the door, window shutters and roof painted green. I went in the door and began climbing.

Ernest Lewis' business card was tacked to the door on the third floor. The door was closed and had a police padlock on it.

I walked back down one flight of stairs and knocked on the second-floor door. It was opened quickly by a stocky, middle-aged woman in dungarees, sweatshirt and apron. She had an artist's brush in her plump hand and her clothes were smeared with various colored paints. She looked out at me hesitantly, almost fearfully.

"I'd like to talk to you about what happened to Ernest Lewis upstairs," I told her.

She sucked in her cheeks and went on eyeing me

uncertainly. "Are you another detective?"

"Uh-huh."

"Oh . . . Well . . . Come in." She backed up to make room for me. Her living room had a couch against one wall; otherwise, its conversion into an artist's studio was complete. Her paintings were all big, wild abstracts. They weren't good, but there were a lot of them, hanging on the walls, leaning against chairs and the couch, and one in the works on an easel by the bay window facing the street.

"I told the other detectives all I could," she said. "There wasn't much to tell, actually. I heard the scream and called the police. You people have been up to Mr. Lewis' apartment. So you know more than I do. I wouldn't go up there for anything."

"Just a couple more questions," I told her. "Lewis took a bad beating before he died. Didn't you hear any of it?"

"No. I told the other detectives. I went to sleep early last night. I didn't hear a thing. Not till that woman screamed and woke me up."

"When was that?"

"One-thirty in the morning. I haven't had any sleep since. I hope I can sleep tonight."

"This woman who screamed," I asked her, "did you get a look at her?"

"Look at her? Of course not. I wouldn't have stuck a foot outside my door for all the money . . ."

"I thought you might have looked out your window and seen her leaving the building. She wasn't there when the officer arrived."

She shook her head. "I didn't stir out of my bed after she let out that awful scream up in Mr. Lewis' apartment. I just picked up the phone by my bed and called the police. And I stayed there in bed till they came. I was scared to death."

"How well did you know Ernest Lewis?"

"Not at all. Not even to say hello to. We just nodded when we ran into each other. That's the nice thing about New York. Everybody respects everybody else's privacy. You know how it is. I'm from Baltimore, myself. I prefer New York. Down in Baltimore . . ."

"Did you ever see Lewis with a girl named Angela?"

"I saw him with different girls, sometimes. But I wouldn't know any of their names."

I described Angela to her, carefully.

She frowned thoughtfully, absently digging paint out from under her fingernails with the sharp end of her paintbrush.

"It could be her," she said finally.

"Tell me."

"Well, I saw a girl who looked something like that. She used to spend the night with Mr. Lewis sometimes. I think so, anyway. I saw her going up to his apartment one evening. And a couple mornings I saw her coming down from his place, once with him. I could see they liked each other."

"You didn't hear him call her by name?"

"No. . . . Is she the one I heard scream?"

"She could be," I told her, and went on trying to pry information out of her. But there wasn't anything else to be got from her. She minded her own business, knew nothing about Lewis except that he was some kind of photographer, and that was that.

Finally she looked at me with a suggestion of suspicion and asked, "Didn't Mr. Lewis' secretary tell you any of these things you're asking me about? Seems to me she'd be the one to know these things."

"His secretary?"

Her suspicion began to form. "Yes. She's up there in his studio on the top floor now, poor thing. The other detectives talked to her. I saw them . . . Don't you people tell each other what's going on? If you're one of them you must . . ."

"You know how it is," I said quickly, winked, and hurried out of her place, leaving her to puzzle out what I'd meant.

I went up the steps, past Lewis' padlocked apartment, up to the top floor. The door there was open. I walked in.

The big, neat photography studio inside was empty. Across the floor a corner was partitioned off as an office. The sound of a drawer being closed came from behind the partition. I crossed the room, looked through the open doorway into the office, which was just big enough to contain its filing cabinets, desk and two chairs. There was a girl standing behind the desk, taking things out of the drawers and stuffing them into the enormous black leather handbag open on top of the desk. They were the kind of things with which a girl stocks any place where she works: Kleenex, an extra lipstick, a comb, a clothes brush, a tin of aspirin, well-worn slippers. . . .

She stopped what she was doing, raised her head and looked across the desk at me. The shock of what had happened to Lewis still showed on her young, pretty face.

"You were Ernest Lewis' secretary?" I asked her.

"Yes." Her voice was almost a whisper, but there was a lot of latent strength behind it.

She was a tiny girl, about five-one. Her face, framed by curly, honey-brown hair, was cute in a snub-nosed, clear-skinned, innocent-wide-blue-eyes way. The desk hid her legs, but the rest of her figure was unusually good for a short girl.

She was used to the kind of male look I was giving her. She let it pass right through her and went on looking at me, waiting.

"What's your name?" I asked her.

"Are you another reporter?"

"I'm a private detective. My name's Jake Barrow.

I'm trying to find out if someone I know is involved in what happened to Lewis."

That bought me some more scrutiny from her. She took her time about it. I put on my most reliable look for her, and she finally decided she could trust me—at least with her name.

"I'm Nel Tarey," she said.

"Nel . . . like in Nellie?"

"I'm afraid so. But if you call me that I'll be your enemy for life."

I laughed and shook my head. "Thanks for warning me. Been working for Lewis long?"

Some horror came back into her blue eyes at the mention of Lewis. Her voice went low again. "No. Just a month. . . . This is my first job in New York. I'm from Chicago. Ernie was a good boss. He . . ." She bit her lower lip and half-closed her eyes. "They made me go in and identify him. . . ." She shuddered, remembering.

"Maybe he was more than just a boss to you?" I suggested.

She opened her eyes all the way and met my stare, not getting sore. "He was just a boss."

"You're a very attractive girl. Lewis was young enough to want to make a try."

"He tried."

"But you kept your virtue intact?"

"I'm not overly worried about my virtue, Mr. Barrow," Nel said simply. "It's just that I didn't like him . . . in that way. As a boss, he was fine. I expect passes. He made his, and when I said no and he saw that I meant it, he let it go at that. . . . What was it you wanted to know, Mr. Barrow?"

"Did Lewis know a girl named Angela?"

"Angela what?"

"All I know is Angela." I described her to Nel Tarey.

Nel shook her head. "No . . . But then I never saw any of his friends. I was only here during working hours."

"Maybe she modeled for him?"

"Ernie didn't use models. He did mostly product photography."

"Did you ever hear him talk to anybody named Angela, on the phone here?"

That got me another shake of her head. She dropped a ballpoint pen in the big handbag and snapped it shut. It bulged with its load.

"Now I'll have to start hunting another job," she said absently. "I really hate job hunting."

"You won't have any trouble finding something else," I told her.

"I guess not. I had a year in a Chicago insurance office before coming here. But I still loath job hunting . . . All those questionnaires to fill out and all."

"Why'd you decide to leave Chicago for New York?"

"More opportunity for advancement here. I don't want to remain a secretary all my life."

I looked around the tiny office. "Not much chance for advancement in this setup."

"Not with Ernie. But it was a way into advertising. I've already learned a lot about his end of it. And I met many of his contacts. Sooner or later one of them would have had a better opening for me."

"Any of these contacts you met have any reason for murdering Lewis?"

I asked it quietly, but it didn't catch her off guard. Her head came up and she eyed me for a moment.

"No, of course not. He didn't have dealings with that sort of people. His business was very respectable."

I sighed. "It's obvious he did something that got him into trouble with some very rough customers, Nel."

"Well whatever it was, I don't know anything

about it. All of his work that I had anything to do with was quite ordinary commercial photography. With respectable people."

"Are you sure you can't think of any reason someone would kill him? Dig into your memory a little more."

"I'm not sure I should," she told me flatly. "I'm not sure I should be talking to you about it at all. I told the police everything I know. Which isn't much. But if you have any right to be asking questions like this, why don't you ask the police? Would they tell you anything?"

"Depends," I told her honestly. "Depends who the cops involved are. Some'll talk to me. Some hate my guts. Do you remember the cop in charge of this one?"

"A detective named Sellers."

"Lieutenant Sellers." I nodded. "We're on good enough terms."

"Then I think," Nel Tarey said, "that you should be asking him your questions."

I shrugged. "Okay. But you've got no reason to be afraid of talking to me, have you?"

"Maybe not. But after what's happened to Ernie, I'd rather play it safe."

She picked up the big handbag and carried it around the desk toward the doorway with her. Her legs were fine; long for her height, and strongly curved.

"Mind giving me your phone number and address," I asked her. "In case I want to talk to you again, after I see Lieutenant Sellers."

She stopped in the doorway and eyed me uncertainly. Finally she shook her head. "I don't think so," she said. "I don't really know you. For all I know you might . . ."

She stopped herself from finishing it. But I had the feeling she was picturing me in the act of murdering Ernest Lewis.

"Okay," I said. "I'll get Lieutenant Sellers to phone you and tell you I'm harmless."

"I wish you would. Then I'll be glad to answer any more questions you want to ask."

"Like whether or not you've got a date tomorrow night?"

That drew a grin out of her. But not a really enthusiastic one. I followed her across the studio to the landing outside. She hurried down the stairs to the pavement as though she were afraid I was going to grab her from behind.

Outside the building, she felt safer about me. She stopped and faced me and said, "I'm sorry if I've been impolite with you, Mr. Barrow. But under the circumstances . . ."

I assured her I understood. She nodded, looked at me for a moment longer, then walked away up the pavement. I turned and headed in the opposite direction. There was a candy store at the end of the block where I could make a phone call to Lieutenant Sellers.

I was halfway to the corner when a Ford sedan detached itself from the curb across the narrow street and went rocketing past me with a squealing of tires.

I spun around, saw that Nel Tarey had stepped off the curb and was crossing the street.

The Ford was aimed at her, gathering speed with every inch of street tar burned under its spinning tires.

FOUR

I yelled at the top of my lungs.

Nel Tarey turned her head, saw the car hurtling at her. She lurched aside, trying desperately to get out of its path, just as it reached her. I saw the side of its fender make contact with her hip.

The fender seemed to just brush her as the Ford roared past. But she was hurled off her feet, flung sprawling in the gutter, on her hands and knees.

The driver of the Ford applied the brakes, hard. The Ford screeched to a jolting halt, fifty yards further on. Nel Tarey was still on her hands and knees near the curb, her head hanging, too dazed to move. The Ford went into reverse, began racing backwards, cutting diagonally across the street to run her over.

By then I had my Magnum out, the safety off. I dropped to my knees and braced my right hand with my left for steady aim and began pumping bullets at the Ford's right rear tire. The heavy gun bucked and roared in my grip five times in rapid succession, the shots blending together in one long, loud explosion.

The tire blew out. The Ford swerved out of control ten feet from Nel Tarey, skidded past her by inches, and crashed backwards into a telephone pole.

I lurched to my feet and started sprinting for the car as one of its front doors was flung open and a man of medium height and build leaped out onto the pavement.

Before I could squeeze off a shot at him, he was across the pavement and out of sight in an alley. I kept running past Nel Tarey and swerved into the alley. A gun cracked from further inside the alley. The bullet ricocheted off the brick wall beside my head, showering brick dust in my eyes. I dropped to a low crouch, blinking my eyes to clear them, firing blindly up the alley.

When I could see again, the alley was empty. I raced down it and found it went all the way through to the next street. There were people there, turning to look at me and the gun in my hand with shocked faces. But the man I was after was gone.

I thumbed the gun on safe and slipped it into the holster under my jacket and hurried back through the alley to Nel Tarey.

She was standing, leaning against the telephone

pole, staring at the Ford, her handbag clutched in both hands and held tight against her stomach. As I came up to her she turned and looked at me. She'd had a full day. First Ernest Lewis, now this. Her wide blue eyes were blank. I reached out a hand to her and she grabbed it, hard. She was shivering uncontrollably.

The Precinct Station Detectives' Room was long, narrow, high-ceilinged, its walls a dirty brown. The bare, black floor was covered with flattened chewing gum wads that had long ago hardened into part of the linoleum. The smell of the disinfectant used in mopping the station hung in the thick, hot air of the room.

Nel Tarey, Lieutenant Sellers and I sat on hard chairs grouped around Sergeant Riley's desk, at the far end of the long room. The room's single tall window was behind Riley's desk, and it was wide open; but no noticeable amount of fresh air came through it. It wouldn't have dared. Flanking the window were an old framed photograph of J. Edgar Hoover and a square, cracked mirror. The faucet of the discolored sink under the mirror leaked steadily, slowly, remorselessly. Riley, in charge of the precinct detectives, seemed to have abandoned all interest in us as soon as Lieutenant Sellers of Homicide had showed up. Leaning back in his swivel chair behind the desk, his plump hands folded on his plump stomach, Riley gazed up at the flyspecks on the ceiling, making a show of not listening. He seemed to be lost in a dream all his own. Judging by the expression on his creased, florid face, the dream wasn't too pleasant. Maybe he was thinking of what he'd like to do to big-wheel homicide cops who horned in on anything interesting enough to get space in the newspapers.

He wasn't bothering Lieutenant Sellers any. Sellers had ignored Riley after a first brief nod on entering the room. He was a tall, thin man in his late thirties, with a pale, freckled face dominated by an unusually large nose. He sat erect and absolutely still on his chair, his whole attention focused on Nel Tarey as she told what had happened.

"He was trying to kill me," she stated determinedly when she finished. She was over her first shock, and some of the blankness had gone out of her eyes. "I'm sure of it. That couldn't have been just drunk driving or anything like that. He was really trying to run me over!"

Lieutenant Sellers nodded. "Sure he was."

"But why?"

"You tell me."

"How can I? I haven't any idea what it's all about."

"Got any enemies, Miss Tarey?"

She looked shocked again. "Of course not."

Sellers nodded again, meaninglessly. "Of course not," he repeated. "So it has to be connected with the Lewis killing. Maybe you know something you didn't tell me this morning."

"I do not," Nel snapped. "I told you every single thing I know."

"Maybe," Sellers said, unperturbed, "you know something without realizing you know it. Or whoever murdered your boss thinks you do."

She shook her head. "I told you everything I could think of when you asked me all those questions before."

"Think about it some more," Sellers suggested. "Maybe something else'll come to you." He looked at me. "Okay, Jake. What's your connection with it?"

I told him about Angela.

He listened, frowning, absorbing and cross-indexing what I told him. It didn't make any lights go on in his eyes. "I haven't come across any dame named Angela so far in this case. But then I haven't had a chance to dig into Lewis' background yet. Maybe I'll turn her up when I do."

"It might just be a coincidence," I said. "She might have meant some other guy named Ernie."

"Sure. But it's worth checking. Suppose you find out what you can dig up on this Angela. And if you make contact with her, grab her for me. I'd like to question her."

"You've got a whole police force to do your checking for you," I told him.

"Like hell I have. Everybody's busy with something else. Including me. I got three other killings I'm assigned to, before this Lewis one. This is a busy town for anybody in the murder business. I could use a little cooperation, Jake."

"I'm being cooperative. What you're asking me to do is work for you. For free. I've got a living to make."

I was going to do what he wanted me to do, anyway. But I wanted him to ask me a few times more. So he'd remember afterwards that he owed me a favor in return whenever I needed his help.

"Jake," Sellers said conversationally, "I was having a talk about you just the other day, down at headquarters. With Lieutenant Flint. I was trying to tell him you're an all right guy. But he still doesn't like you very much."

"Flint and I have a personal beef."

"He's pretty highly thought of, around the Homicide Bureau. When you've got a cop like him against you, a guy in your line of work can use another cop that's on your side. Like me."

I heaved a resigned sigh. "Okay. I'll try to locate Angela for you."

"Thought you would, a nice guy like you . . . By the way, this character that dragged her into that alley, could he have been the same guy that tried to run Miss Tarey down?"

"No. The other one was big. Real big. The one with the Ford was average size and build."

"That's a real dandy description, Jake. A lot to go

on. You couldn't add just a little more to it, could you? Or did he just have an average face, too?"

"I didn't get enough of a look at his face to tell you anything," I said.

"Swell . . ." Sellers looked at Nel Tarey. "How about you? See his face?"

She shook her head. "I didn't see him at all. Just that car, coming at me."

Sellers laced his long, thin fingers together and cracked the knuckles, the first sign he'd given so far of being under any kind of tension. "How're you coming at remembering something you might have forgotten to tell me this morning?"

"There's nothing more to remember. I told you everything. I never heard him say anything on the phone that sounded like someone was threatening him. Nobody ever came to the studio and threatened him or even acted angry with him."

The phone on Detective Sergeant Riley's desk rang. He picked it up lazily, still gazing dreamily at the ceiling, and barked his name into the mouthpiece.

After that he listened a while, then growled, "Like I figured," and hung up.

"The Ford ain't going to help," he said, to no one in particular. "Belongs to a woman runs a candy store. She reported it stolen an hour before it was used to try killing Miss Tarey."

Sellers slapped his hands on his long thighs and stood up. "Well . . . that's that. Miss Tarey, somebody tried to kill you, and may try again. It'd be safer if you didn't stay in your apartment for a while. Until we clear this up. Better move somewhere else for a few days, and don't let too many people know where."

"Move . . ." She murmured.

"Just temporarily. Any place, so long as you don't leave town. Got any friends you can move in with?"

"None of my friends have an apartment big

enough . . . How about a hotel?"

"That'd be fine," Sellers told her. "Make it in some other part of town. And call and leave a message at my desk, letting me know where to get in touch with you . . . I'd go along with you for protection while you're packing your things, only I'm snowed under right now." He looked at me.

I nodded. "I'll go with her."

I looked at her. "Unless you're still afraid of me?"

"You saved my life," she said quietly and let it go at that.

We caught a cruising cab outside the station and rode to her place. She had an apartment over a movie theater near Fourteenth and Seventh. I took a quick look around as we got out of the cab. There didn't seem to be anybody watching her place. I led the way into the building, and kept my eyes and ears alert. My nerves were taut; I didn't have to work at keeping them that way.

There was nobody waiting inside the entry, on the inner stairs, or up in the second floor corridor. We stopped in front of her door. She started fishing in the big handbag for her keys.

I glanced at the door. I wasn't looking for anything special. But the marks were there, clearly visible in the wood beside the door lock.

Stiffening, I put my hand on Nel's shoulder other and gripped hard enough to alert her. I reached my hand under my lapel and took out the Magnum.

Her eyes went big and round. I pushed her gently aside, past the place where the door hinged to the wall. Her mouth opened, but she saw the look on my face and didn't speak. I let go of her and tried the door-knob, very carefully.

It wasn't locked. It had been jimmied open.

FIVE

I shoved the door hard enough so it would swing all the way and hit the wall inside. I went in fast while it was still swinging. The living room was small, tidy, and empty. I kept going, past a tiny kitchen, into the bedroom. I checked the closets and the bathroom. There was no one in the apartment.

Holstering the gun, I hurried back to Nel Tarey. "Okay. You can come in now."

Her face was strained. "What . . ."

"Somebody jimmied your door open. Whoever did it is gone."

"What does it mean?" she whispered.

"I'd guess the guy that wants you dead was waiting here for you, and got tired of waiting. Come on. It's safe now."

She walked into the living room with the slow, awkward, jolting steps of a drunk trying not to stagger. I followed her, closing the apartment door. She went into the tiny kitchen, opened a cabinet and took out a small bottle of Scotch. I watched her pour a tumbler a quarter full, drink it all with shuddering gulps. She washed it down with cold water from the tap, then stood there a while with the empty glass in her hand, staring at the wall.

Finally she put the glass down and turned to look at me.

"I'm all right now," she said. But her voice was still a bit shaky. "Someone is trying to kill me, Jake. What am I going to do?"

"First you look around, see if anything is missing. It could have been a burglar."

"I don't have anything worth stealing." But she went for a look around, anyway.

It didn't take long. The apartment was quite small, and neat enough so she could have noticed at once if anything had been disturbed. When she was finished looking, she shook her head. "Nothing is touched." She sat on the edge of a two-seater sofa slipcovered in dark red. Her fingers twitched at the material.

"What time did you leave here this morning?" I asked her.

"I didn't," she said, without looking up. "That's one of the things the police asked me. They wanted to know where I was when Ernie was murdered. I . . . I wasn't here last night. At all."

The first faint suspicion skittered like a spider through my guts. I didn't let it into my voice. "Where were you?"

"I left here last night before midnight, to see a girl friend of mine off on a plane to Paris. The plane was delayed in taking off. I waited with her at Idlewild."

"Till when?"

"The plane didn't take off till seven this morning. I spent the whole night with her in the airport waiting room. It was her first flight and she was nervous about it. So I stayed there with her. Then after she left at seven, I wasn't able to get a cab till almost eight. So I went straight to Ernie's studio. The police were there when I got there. And Ernie . . . dead in his apartment."

I considered it for a moment. "I'd bet your door was jimmied last night some time. You can thank the late take off of your friend's plane for saving your life."

"I feel like I'm in some kind of nightmare," she murmured. She took a deep breath and her head came up till she was looking into my eyes. "You're a private detective. People hire private detectives to protect them, don't they?"

"When they need protection and can afford it."

"Can I hire you? Until the police catch . . . whoever it is?"

"I didn't know you had that kind of money."

"I've got a little in the bank. I saved it from my job in Chicago. Would it cost very much to hire you?"

"You've already got me. Use the money for a hotel room. That'll be the only protection you need. I know a good hotel that won't be too expensive. I'll make sure nobody follows us there, and you'll register under a false name. Then all you have to do is sit tight in your room till things are straightened out. I know the house detective there. He'll keep an eye on you."

"What am I supposed to do, stay cooped up there and never go out?"

I nodded. "Watch TV. Have your meals sent up. Don't phone anybody and don't tell anybody where you are."

"Sounds like a lovely way," she said, mournfully, "to go crazy."

"I'll drop in and keep you company from time to time."

She forced a grin. "That's a mighty sneaky way of getting a girl all to yourself, Jake." The banter in her voice was forced, too.

"I hadn't thought about it that way," I told her. I looked down at her soft fullness. "A nice thought, though."

She blushed, but she didn't take her eyes from mine as she stood up. "I'll pack a suitcase," she said, softly. "Be with you in a minute."

She was almost as good as her word. Ten minutes later we were out on the pavement, hailing a cab. No one tailed us away from her place. I made sure of that.

We were lucky to have caught the cab when we did. A few minutes later it finally began to rain, hard and steady with drops as big as ice-cubes. It took over a half-hour for our cab to work its way through the wet snarl up to the hotel. The place was a couple blocks off Central Park West, a residential hotel with a few rooms for transients. We ducked out of the cab, under the sidewalk canopy, and hurried into the lobby. While Nel registered under a false name and followed a bell-hop up to her room, I went into the cubbyhole office of the house man, a beefy ex-cop with sharp eyes, named MacLevy.

I told MacLevy about Nel Tarey and said he should check it with Lieutenant Sellers at Homicide. MacLevy didn't act very excited about it. Ex-cops don't excite worth a damn. But he said he'd keep a check on her. I left his cubbyhole and went up in the elevator to see Nel.

She had her suitcase open on the bed and was trans-ferring her things from it to the closet and bureau.

"The room okay?" I asked her.

"It's not exactly home, but it'll do." She went on emptying her suitcase in an abstracted manner.

I picked up the room phone and asked for the num-ber of my answering service. The word there was that I'd still had no calls of importance. I hung up and looked at Nel, who was dumping her empty suitcase on the floor of the closet. "Well, I'd better be going now."

A scared look came over her fresh young face again. She came to me quickly, her small hands clutching my wrists. "Please. Don't go yet. Stay and have something to eat with me, at least."

I suddenly realized that I was hungry, so I agreed. We ordered our lunches sent up to her room. I finished off mine, but Nel just fiddled with hers. She was still too upset to eat. She'd thought about the meal only as an excuse to keep me there with her a little longer. But by the time we'd finished our coffee she had a better grip on herself and was about as calm as I could expect.

When I went to the window and looked out, I saw that the rain had stopped and patches of bright late-afternoon sunshine gleamed on the roofs.

I turned away from the window and told her,

"Now I do have to be going."

She sighed. "I suppose so." She walked me to the door of her room, stopped there with me, facing me. "Dammit!" she said softly. "Why'd this have to happen to me?"

"Take it easy," I told her. "It'll be over soon. Maybe sooner than that, if I have a little luck."

She eyed me and came closer, till the breasts pushing out the front of her blouse were touching me. "Just remember, you promised to come back and keep me company when you can. I'm not built to be a hermit for long."

"I'll vouch for that," I told her, and seized by an impulse that was not very sudden I leaned down and lightly kissed her pouting lips.

She didn't flinch away or look surprised. She'd been expecting it.

Knoble's Gym was a wide, hulking four-storey dirty brick building a few blocks from Madison Square Garden. In that block the windows of the barbershop, the diner, the saloons and the men's clothing store all displayed framed and autographed photographs of bygone champions trying to look friendly and human. The block was on the edge of Hell's Kitchen, one of the slum sections that supplies a steady stream of raw material for the fight game. A lot of the kids from there had made Knoble's Gym their first stop on a road they hoped would take them a few blocks farther to bigtime fights at the Garden.

Most of them got a taste of ring punishment and quit for less strenuous work, or to peddle their muscle to the mobs. Some went on taking it, in fifty-buck tank-town fights, and wound up as punchy flotsam. A few actually made it to the top. Steve Canby's middleweight, Frankie Sims, was the latest of these. According to the sports writers, Sims was going to make it all the way to the championship.

A big red-and-black poster which advertised Friday's Garden fight between Frankie Sims and Rocky Gabe was tacked to one of the wooden walls inside the building's recessed doorway. I went in past it, giving a buck to the guy guarding the entrance. Once he'd been a heavyweight contender. Now he served as general handyman and janitor around the gym. The vague eyes in his battered face blinked at me and he mumbled something. I think he was thanking me for the dollar bill. It had taken the doctor three hours to bring him to after his last fight, and only a few close bar pals could understand anything he mumbled anymore.

I climbed the narrow, dirty wooden steps inside. Halfway up the strong smells of sweat, liniment and leather reached down and grabbed me by the nose.

The second floor was one huge room filled with training fighters and spectators. Besides the four warriors pounding each other in the two regulation-size rings dominating the center of the room, there were over fifteen others scattered around skipping rope, punching bags, shadow-boxing. The room was thick with cigar smoke and voices and the sounds of leather-padded blows landing on flesh, the delicate flicking of skipping ropes against the wooden floor, the staccato drumming of punching bags.

I collared a gloomy-looking, pasty-faced fight promoter and asked him where I'd find Steve Canby.

He glanced furtively behind him, then whispered confidentially, "Top floor." It's ingrained in fight circles; even if a guy is only telling you the time, he'll act like he's revealing that the champ is planning to take a dive.

I climbed the steps to the top floor. The room there was smaller, with a single ring in the center of it, surrounded by rows of folding chairs taken up with spectators silently watching Frankie Sims work out with a sparring partner. A few of the spectators were sports reporters. But the rest were all members of the upper echelons of the fight racket, wearing the loud, expensive suits and pale, passionless faces of their profession.

Steve Canby stood on the ring apron by one of the posts, his sharp-featured, perpetually anxious face turned toward his fighter inside the ring. Beside him his trainer, Doug McAfee, leaned against the ring post, the relaxed pose of his big, massive-shouldered figure belied by the furrowed concentration on his heavy, thick-featured face. McAfee had been a promising heavyweight, till he'd lost an eye in a fight five years before. Since then he'd surprised a business in which the fundamental stupidity of fighters is usually taken for granted, by proving himself one of the smartest trainers around town.

I stood against the wall watching Frankie Sims show his stuff in the ring. He had plenty to show. He was tall and rangy for a middleweight with slim, smooth muscles rippling under his skin. His face was just a shade lighter than his short-cropped black hair, and he'd been lucky that so far his clean-cut, handsome features hadn't been ruined by scar tissue. He moved as though he were constructed mostly of well-oiled springs.

His sparring partner was shorter, heavier, more solidly muscled. And he wasn't just acting as a punching bag; he was doing his best to pulverize Sims with powerhouse punches. His punches didn't land very often, and never solidly. Frankie Sims evaded those fists as though he were half greyhound, half rabbit, all the time snaking his left unerringly against the sparring partner's flattened, blood-dripping nose.

I'd seen pictures of Frankie Sims outside the ring; he'd always looked like a good-natured young boy. But now, inside the ring, he looked about as good-natured as a starving tiger.

As I watched, Sims suddenly feinted at his sparring partner's belly, making him drop his guard. Sim's right flashed up in an overhand chop that landed flush on the side of the other man's jaw.

I'd read that Frankie Sims could hit. He could. His sparring partner went off his feet as though he'd run full-tilt against a stone wall. He landed on his back and stayed there, blinking up at the ceiling, his breath whistling through his open mouth. Not out, but just suddenly very weary.

"Okay!" Doug McAfee barked. "That's all for today, Frankie."

The sparring partner sighed with heavy relief, rolled tiredly over on his side, got his hands and knees under him. Frankie Sims, looking like a good-natured kid again, hurried over to help raise his sparring partner to his feet. Doug McAfee climbed through the ropes and wrapped a thick terrycloth robe around Sims's sweat-streaked figure, led him out of the ring toward the dressing room. The spectators began moving out of their chairs, speaking to each other in the usual furtive whispers. I pushed through them to Steve Canby, who was climbing down off the edge of the apron.

We shook hands. Canby managed to look glad to see me.

"Your boy looks great," I told him.

He ran a hand over his thinning hair and for a moment a pleased grin replaced his usual worried look. "Yeah. He does, don't he? You come over to see if you should bet on him? We got it in the bag."

I shook my head. "Something else, Steve. Let's talk private."

He looked worried again. But he said, "Sure," and led the way to one of the tall open windows set in one wall. He hooked a leg over the window and climbed out. I followed him onto the rickety fire escape platform.

He lit a cigarette and took a deep drag of smoke, gazing down at the street below. "I know we're gonna win," he muttered, mostly to himself. "But my guts always get tight this close to a big-money fight like this one. I can't help it. Don't even feel like eating at all." He shook his head to dispel the disturbing thoughts of his troubled stomach and looked at me. "What'd you want to talk about?"

"Know a woman named Angela?"

He didn't have to think about it. "Sure. Angela Hart. She who you mean?"

I described her. He nodded. "Yeah. That's Angela."

"Know her pretty well?" I asked him.

"Well enough. She used to be a cigarette girl at the Oran Club. Till she quit to work as a model in the garment industry, some place on Seventh Avenue."

"Seen her or heard from her today?"

"No. Why should I?" There was a sharp, guarded note in his voice.

"She came into the Oran Club last night," I told him. "After you left. She was looking for you."

"Well, I haven't seen her. Why're you asking about her?"

"I think she's in trouble."

"What kind of trouble?"

"I'm not sure," I told him, watching his face.

He flicked his smoked-down cigarette away from the fire escape, watched it arc downward and bounce in the middle of the street below. Then he looked at me, his sharp face hard. "Five'll get you twenty it's man trouble."

"Why do you say that?"

"Because I know her, that's why." Some anger had crept into his voice. "She's a tramp, a nympho. She's always had too many guys on the string at the same time."

He took out another cigarette and started to light

it. I watched him change his mind, toss cigarette and match over the rusty rail of the fire escape. Then he told me, "As a matter of fact, I used to be one of them. One of her men. Until I found out how much company I had." His face twisted suddenly with the angry memory. Then he shrugged and laughed half-heartedly. "I got pretty sore about it for a while. I'd been damn hot for her. But then I figured what the hell, there're too many broads in the world to get an ulcer over Angela. So I stopped messing around with her."

"You seem to've done pretty well without her," I said. "If that sexy dancer you took out last night is a sample."

He grinned, pleased. "Yeah. Boy, I'm gonna miss that little baby. Maybe I'll fly down to Cuba to see her, after the fight."

His face went dreamy with anticipation. I brought him back to me with: "How long ago did you bust up with Angela Hart?"

"Oh . . . about five, six months ago, I guess."

"And you haven't seen her, since?"

"Oh, I've seen Angela a few times since then, once I got over being sore at her. When she was broke and she'd come around wanting to borrow a little scratch. I'm a sucker for a touch, you know me."

I nodded.

"I'll bet," he said, "that's why she was looking for me last night. To hit me for a loan again."

It fitted. She'd told me she needed money to get out of town. "Could be," I said.

"Sure . . . That gal's got one hell of a nerve. She borrows, but she never pays it back. How come you're suddenly so interested in Angela?" Then he thought about it and leered at me. "Or should I ask?"

"You can ask. She was in some kind of jam. I wanted to help her. Only she ran out on me."

Canby grinned nastily. "Too bad. She probably found another guy. That's the way she is."

"Would you know where she lives these days?"

He scratched his chin with a bitten-down thumb-nail. "Well . . . I ain't sure, now. Haven't seen Angela in over a month. But last I knew, she was living in a jazzy apartment house over on the East Side. Maybe she's moved out by now, though. Rent's real steep in places like that."

I got the address of the apartment building from Canby and left him. When I reached the pavement out-side the gym, I looked up. Canby was still on the fire escape, leaning with his elbows on the rail, looking down. He raised a hand to me.

At the end of the block, I went into a diner phone booth and called the apartment building Canby had told me about. The switchboard operator told me that Angela Hart still lived there. But she hadn't been in or called in since yesterday evening.

I took a cab to my apartment and called my answer-ing service. There'd been some calls for me, but none of them important, and no call from Angela Hart.

I wandered aimlessly around my apartment for a while, thinking of all that had happened since I first laid eyes on Angela Hart in the early dark hours that morning. I told myself she was far out of New York by now, headed for Mexico. I told myself she was nothing of the kind. She was still right here in town, hiding somewhere; she'd been phoning me all day, and hadn't thought of phoning my office when she couldn't get me. I told myself that even if I heard from her, it would turn out that the Ernie she'd referred to wasn't the murdered one, and that the trouble she was in would have no connection with the trouble Nel Tarey was in.

I told myself to stop telling myself things when I didn't know what I was talking about.

I went into the kitchenette and gazed at the two bottles of Chartreuse—the 86 proof yellow bottle, and the 110 proof green bottle. A bunch of monks in a

French monastery make Chartreuse from a secret recipe that makes Georgia corn liquor seem as mild as Coca-Cola in comparison. It's too strong to drink more than a few drops at a swallow, and once inside you it heats like a furnace and hits like a pile driver. But it also has the effect of sharpening my thinking.

I drank a little of the 110 proof green. It worked. My thoughts stopped being confused. They became sharp and clear as icicles. But they still didn't add up to anything.

I wandered back into the living room and stared at the books in the bookcase, searching for something to pass the time with. I finally took out volume two of *Mendel's Medical Classification of Bullet Wounds* and settled down in the wing chair by the window with it. I read through a complete chapter of it. The phone still hadn't rung.

I dropped Mendel on the floor beside my chair and smoked and watched the shadows of evening thicken into night outside my window. When it was completely dark outside, I realized it was also completely dark inside. I got up and turned on a couple lamps. Then I phoned down to the diner for a meal.

I was just finishing dinner when the phone rang.

I knocked over my chair getting to the phone. I snatched it up and barked, "Yeah?" into the mouthpiece.

The voice in my ear whispered, "Jake?"

It was Angela Hart.

SIX

"Jake," she pleaded over the phone, "I need help. Bad." Her voice was shaky, and slurred as though she'd had too much to drink.

"Why'd you run out on me?"

"I had to. They came for me. Right after you got

that phone call and left your apartment."

"They?" I asked her.

"Two men. I looked out the window right after you left and saw a car pull up and saw them get out. One of them was the man who tried to kill me."

Through the phone connection, I heard her draw a long, shuddering breath before she went on, "I was so scared . . . I got out of your apartment fast, before they came in the building. I rushed up the stairway to the floor above your apartment and stayed there till they left."

"You're sure they were after you?"

"Of course they were! I heard them go in your apartment, Jake. I'd forgotten to lock the door when I ducked out. After they left I went back down and wrote a note for you and got out of there. I figured it wasn't safe for me. They knew I was there. They might come back. . . . Jake, you've got to help me!"

"I can't, till you tell me what it's all about," I told her.

"I will. I . . . I need help to get away, Jake. Please come right away. Then I'll tell you about it."

"Where are you?"

She was in a fleabag hotel on the West Side, up near the edge of Harlem. "I'm registered as Joan Smith," she told me. "But you come right up to my room, 414. I'll be waiting here for you."

It wasn't till after I'd hung up the phone that I remembered that the last time she'd said that—that she'd be waiting for me—I'd come back here to my apartment to find her gone.

It was just a passing thought. I wouldn't call it a premonition.

Except for the theater district, early night traffic in Manhattan is a lot lighter than by day. So I got in my Chevy and drove uptown. Or started to. I was about halfway there when the car ran out of gas and stopped, right in the middle of the street.

I hadn't bothered to glance at the gas gauge when I got in. There'd been no need to. The tank had been more than half full the previous night. I distinctly remembered that.

Now, with the Chevy stalled in the middle of the street and other cars honking their horns angrily as they swung around from behind me, I looked at the gasoline indicator. The needle was pointing to dead-empty. I hadn't smelled gas when I got in, the way I would have if the tank had been punctured. So someone had siphoned it out.

It happens like that around New York every day—guys getting gas free by siphoning it out of parked cars. Only I didn't think that was what had happened this time.

I got out of the Chevy and pushed it to the curb. Setting the hand brake, I hurried away in search of a cab. I walked seven blocks before an empty one cruised by. The delay had cost me fifteen minutes. In all, it was over a half-hour from the time I left my apartment till I reached the hotel where Angela Hart was waiting for me.

I've seen worse-looking hotels, but not lately. The block it was in was caught between a tenement neighborhood and an area being rehabilitated with new economy apartment buildings to replace the slums. The block next to it had an apartment project halfway built. In the block that contained the hotel, half the buildings were already abandoned and boarded up in preparation for the wreckers.

The hotel itself was a narrow six-storey stone building whose original color had long ago vanished under layers of soot. I went through the door into a small lobby with cracked linoleum floor. Across the room from the entrance was a single ancient elevator with an iron-grille door. A row of wooden folding chairs against the left wall took the place of a sofa. There was a recessed alcove in the right wall, with a wide wooden desk in it and a man sitting behind the desk.

He had his hands folded peacefully on top of the desk and he turned his head and looked at me without interest as I came in. His face was narrow and pinched above his neat bow tie.

"Can I help you?" he said without undue politeness.

I nodded at the elevator. "Self service?"

"No. I take you up." He stood up and came around from behind the desk. He wore a new-looking dark blue linen suit that hung very nattily on his average build, making him look stronger than he was. I followed him to the elevator.

"Which floor?" he asked in a bored voice as we got in.

"Fourth."

He nodded, clanked the door shut and shoved the lever over, sending the elevator on its slow, jolting journey upward. At the fourth floor, he had to jiggle the lever back and forth several times before he got the floor of the elevator level with the floor of the corridor.

He pulled the door open and looked at me. "Fourth." His eyes looked like those of a butcher about to feed a slab of meat into the grinder to make hamburger.

I could be wrong. Maybe he was new at the job of running the elevator. Maybe his expensive-looking suit was a present from a rich uncle. Maybe the slight bulge weighing down the right-hand pocket of his jacket was a pipe. If I was wrong, I'd apologize.

I took a step as though I were going to go past him into the corridor. Instead, I balled my fist, swivelled on my heel, and hit him in the temple. Just hard enough to daze him.

He fell back against the side of the elevator, his knees bent, and he started to sag downward, his eyes closing. Halfway down he stopped sagging. When his eyes snapped open he found himself staring at the gun in my fist.

"Yell," I said softly, "and I blow your head off."

His mouth fell open. He straightened up slowly, still leaning against the elevator wall, eyes blinking as they went on staring at my gun. "What is . . ."

I reached into his jacket pocket and dragged out a snub-nosed .32 revolver with its front sight filed off. "Standard equipment for all the room clerks in this hotel?"

He tried to look indignant and sincere at the same time. "We get holdups in this neighborhood," he said. "Is that what this is?"

"You tell me." I caught his thin wrist with my left hand and gave it a hard twist that made him gasp and spin around till his back was toward me. I dragged his wrist up between his shoulder blades in a tight hammerlock.

"Room 414," I told him. "Lead the way. And no noise unless you'd like your spine shot in half."

We went out of the elevator together, up the narrow, rugless, dark corridor past peeling painted doors. We stopped in front of the door with 414 painted in black on the panel.

I strengthened the hammerlock I had on him and touched the small of his back with the muzzle of the Magnum. "Knock," I whispered to the back of his head.

Sweat beaded the back of his neck between the hairline and his collar.

I pressed the gun harder against his spine. "Knock."

He reached a trembling hand out slowly, rapped the door with his knuckles, dropped his arm instantly as though he'd touched fire.

Inside the room, the door lock was snapped. The knob started to turn.

The man between me and the door couldn't stand

it any longer. I saw it coming. His shoulders hunched and even the hammerlock didn't stop his terrified warning yell: "Joe!"

I kicked open the door, still holding him in front of me. The door bounded inward revealing a completely dark room. Before I could make a move a gun exploded in that darkness inside.

The guy I was holding in the hammerlock jarred back against me as the bullet thudded into his chest. Before he could fall out of my grip I shoved him as hard as I could, throwing him away from me in through the open door of the dark room and leaping in, crouched behind him. Another shot rocked the room as I got inside and flung myself to one side. My left hand hit the wall switch inside the doorway, flooding the room with light from a ceiling lamp.

The fake room clerk was sprawling to the floor as the light snapped on. The man inside the room with the .45 in his hand was the big, brutal-faced thug I'd stopped from strangling Angela. His eyes, used to the darkness in the room, blinked with momentary blindness as the sudden light hit them.

Before his eyes could blink open again I squeezed the trigger of the Magnum. It boomed like a cannon in that room. The big slug caught him low. He bent and went to his knees, his mouth straining wide open with his agony. But the .45 didn't fall out of his big hand. He tried to bring it up to fire at me. I shot him in the shoulder, twisting him around sideways against the edge of the room's single bed. He stayed that way and went on concentrating on the .45 in his hand, slowly bringing it around toward me like it weighed a ton. I put the third bullet in his head. His arms dropped instantly. His big body sagged, balanced for a moment on his spread knees, then toppled sideways to the floor.

Dragging in a long, shuddering breath of air laden with burnt gunpowder fumes, I glanced at the fake room clerk sprawled inside the doorway. There was no more life in him than in a pile of old clothes.

Then I looked at Angela Hart. She lay face down on the bed in her pale blue sweater and slacks. There was no need to go closer to her. A lead-weighted black-jack lay on the pillow beside her dark black hair. It had been used to cave in the back of her skull.

SEVEN

I spent what seemed like a long time at the room's open window, staring out at dark nothing and sucking warm outside air into my lungs. When I was sure my stomach was going to behave, I mopped my face and hands with a handkerchief and turned around. There didn't seem to be any phone in the room. I didn't look very hard. I went out of the room, down the corridor to the elevator, and took it down to the lobby.

The hotel's room clerk lay on the floor behind the alcove desk, his wrists and ankles bound together behind him with wire and a surgical-tape gag over his mouth. He was a frail old man in rumpled slacks and a polo shirt.

I knelt beside him and untied him, stripped the tape away from his mouth. He hadn't been hurt. He started talking the second I got the gag off, gasping for breath between every other word.

"Them two jumped me before I knew what they was up to. The bastards tied me up. Old man like me. Gagged me."

I helped him into the chair behind the desk. "Know 'em?"

"Sonsabitches like that? Hell no. Grab me. Tie me up. Shoved me down on the floor. Tell me to stay still or they'll kick my head in." His eyes were blazing with fury. "Bastards like that're ruining this town. Oughta do to 'em like in the old days. Take 'em down to the station, work 'em over with a rubber hose. See how they like it. Pushin' a guy like me around . . ."

He was still at it when I picked up the desk phone, called Homicide, and asked for Lieutenant Sellers.

The police came in dribbles, and kept coming till the place swarmed with them. First a couple uniformed prowl car boys. Then the captain of the local station with three of his precinct detectives. Lieutenant Sellers came in with two other Homicide cops a few minutes after the Emergency Squad truck arrived. They were followed by an ambulance, a police photographer, two men from Fingerprints, the captain of that Detective District, an assistant from the Medical Examiner's office, a detective stenographer, and an Assistant District Attorney with one of the D.A.'s investigators. And between the arrivals of these various branches of the law, the reporters filtered in to swell the ranks.

They all went up to the fourth floor, sweeping with them clusters of excited tenants of the hotel. The aged room clerk went up with them. I stayed in the lobby. I knew what was up there and they could have it. I'd been there.

I sat on the edge of the alcove desk and waited, while the single prowl car cop who'd been stationed in the lobby eyed me uncertainly, not sure if he was supposed to be guarding me. I smoked and looked at the folding chairs against the opposite wall and thought about how nice it would be to go wash all this off me with a long swim in the surf at Jones Beach.

There were five crushed-out cigarette stubs on the floor around my shoes by the time Lieutenant Sellers finally came back down to the lobby with one of his sidekicks, the Assistant D.A., and one of the local precinct squad detectives, trailed by the detective stenographer from Homicide.

"You were right about the girl," Sellers told me. "Angela Hart. Identification's in her handbag. How about the two guys? Did you know 'em?"

I shook my head. "The big one's the guy I caught trying to kill her in that alley. I think the other one might have been the driver of that Ford that tried to run down Nel Tarey. I could be wrong about that. Outside of that, I don't know them."

"Well, we've got the advantage on you there," Sellers said. "We know them. Joe Mardo and Felix Johnston. Heavies for hire by anybody with the dough. I've already got some men out checking on whom they were working for this time."

He sighed heavily, flexed his thin shoulders and cracked his knuckles to ease his tension. "Okay. Now tell us the whole works."

I told them everything that had happened. In detail. The detective stenographer's pencil flew across the pages of his notebook, taking it all down in shorthand.

When I was finished, Sellers held out a hand to me. "I'll have to take your gun. Evidence."

I gave him the Magnum.

"Now," he said, "we go down to headquarters."

"One thing before we leave," I said.

"Yeah?"

"Have somebody check on the phone in my apartment. I think it was tapped."

"Why do you think that?"

"They didn't know where she was till I did. I figure the gas was siphoned out of my car so they could beat me here. They listened in on her call, got here first and killed her, then waited to get me. Probably figuring she might have told me something when I was with her last night."

Sellers nodded at his sidekick, who went to the desk phone to call in for a check on my phone. I followed Sellers out to his car.

He didn't say anything for a while as he drove us downtown. Finally he rumbled disgustedly, "I have all the luck. I was hoping this Angela dish would help me clear up the Ernest Lewis murder. Now whoever did it got her, too, and all I've got out of it is another murder on my workload."

"The Ernie she mentioned to me could still be some other guy," I pointed out. "The two murders might not have anything to do with each other."

"They do, though," Sellers said, flatly. "I told you I might run across her name when I began digging into Lewis' background. I did. Her last name being Hart clinches it."

He told me about it. Both Angela Hart and Ernest Lewis had been involved with a murder that had occurred four months before. A wealthy Seventh Avenue garment manufacturer named Roland Miller had been found in an alley one morning, dead from the blow of some blunt instrument that had caved in his forehead. Despite the fact that any money Miller was carrying on him at the time was missing, the investigating detectives thought it might not be just a simple robbery killing.

It seemed that Roland Miller, a married man with no children, had been spending most of his nights before his murder with Angela Hart. She'd gotten a job as a clothes model in his firm. And it wasn't long before she'd quit her job and Roland Miller had set her up in a two-room suite in the luxury apartment building that was still her address. It was only a few weeks after Miller had started paying her rent that he had been killed. The cops questioned Angela. But she had an alibi.

"Ernest Lewis was her alibi," Lieutenant Sellers told me. "Both he and Angela Hart swore they'd been together the whole night Miller was killed. Seems Miller couldn't satisfy her all by himself and she'd gone to Lewis' apartment. Anyway, the boys couldn't dig up any solid motive for Angela Hart wanting to kill a guy that was keeping her in style, so they had to let it go at that."

The cops had also dug a little into the possible motive of jealousy on the part of Roland Miller's wife. But
they didn't get anywhere in that direction, either. So
they'd finally put down Miller's death as another of the
long list of unsolved New York robbery-murders.

"You agree with that?" I asked Sellers.

He shrugged beside me. "Wasn't my case. Besides,
there wasn't anything to indicate there was more to it
than that." He paused, and then added, "At the time."

"Yeah. But now Angela Hart and Ernest Lewis are
both dead. Both murdered."

Sellers nodded. "Makes you think," he said softly.
"Doesn't it?"

"What about this Roland Miller's wife?" I asked,
"If she found out about her husband and Angela . . ."

"There's nothing in that," Sellers told me slowly.
And then he turned and looked at me. "At least, not
for me. She's money. She knows big people who know
bigger people."

"Oh. It's like that."

"Like that," Sellers said flatly. "The boys that were
on the Roland Miller case found out. They bothered
her a while, and got told to drop it. They dropped it."

"Cover-up?"

"No. I don't think so. If they'd found out anything
at all that made Miller's wife a possible suspect, they
couldn't have dropped it. Nobody's that important."

He parked at the curb in back of the Headquarters
Building and we went inside and up the elevator to
Sellers' office in the Homicide Bureau. There was word
waiting for us when we arrived. The detective who
checked my building found indications that my phone
had been tapped. But the tap wires were gone, and
there was no way now of finding out where they had
led to.

I went into Sellers' office with him, and a few
minutes later a police stenographer entered carrying a

heavy wire-recorder. I made my detailed statement of what had happened all over again, into the recorder. Then I waited around for the statement to be typed up so I could sign it.

The waiting dragged on. Lieutenant Sellers was out of his office more than he was in. Most of the time I sat there in the chair beside his desk alone, smoking and staring at the big map of Manhattan tacked to his wall.

Finally Sellers, after an absence of over an hour, came into his office, closed the door behind him, and slumped down in his chair behind the desk. "I'm bushed," he growled. "Just plain bushed."

"I'm not exactly feeling in my prime, myself. How long's it take to type up a statement around here?"

"You think that's all anybody's got to do?" Sellers snarled at me. "There's so goddam much paper work to be done on a case like this that we're all wading through work up to our eyeballs."

"I've heard the song before."

"It's true! There's just too much work for the size force we got. We need more cops."

"There's already twenty-four thousand cops in New York. Any more and everybody else'd have to move out to make room for them."

"We need more," Sellers insisted. "Christ, there's eight million people in this town, not counting commuters. And the kind of people they are . . . Ah-h, the hell with it."

We sat and looked unpleasantly at each other for a time. Finally, he glanced at his closed door and back to me. Then he opened a drawer of his desk and took out a flat pint of whiskey. "How about you?"

I nodded. "I could use it."

"Get the cups."

I went to the water cooler in one corner of the room and took two paper cups from the dispenser, set them on the desk in front of him. He poured them full. We emptied them slowly, in silence.

Sellers filled both cups again. He picked his up, sipped at it, and leaned back in his chair, some of the nervous fatigue gone from his face.

"A couple of the boys," he said quietly, "went over to have a look at Angela Hart's apartment. Real classy joint. She paid four hundred bucks a month for rent. What do you think of that?"

"Does it have gold wallpaper?"

"It's got a view of the East River. That costs, these days."

"Our place had a view of the East River, where I lived when I was a kid," I told him. "I think my father paid fifteen bucks a month rent, when he could pay it. Two rooms. Same river."

"Sure," Sellers said. "But I'll bet you didn't appreciate the view. You got to pay four hundred a month to really appreciate it." He shook his head. "Four hundred bucks a month! Christ, you know what I get paid a month?"

"Don't start on that again," I told him, and finished the whiskey in my paper cup.

He sighed, sipped from his cup, and looked into it for awhile. Then he looked up at me. "Guess what the boys found in her apartment."

"I give up."

"There's a closet in her bedroom, with a mirror set on the outside of its door. There was some cardboard tacked to the inside of the door. Didn't look right, for a classy apartment like that. So one of the boys pulled the cardboard off, and what do you think?"

I waited.

"Somebody had cut away part of the wood in the door, right behind that mirror. It's a two-way mirror."

I sat up straighter.

He nodded at me. "Yeah. Anybody in the bedroom would see only his reflection in that mirror. But anyone inside the closet could look through that hole in the door, and see through the other side of the trick mirror, into the bedroom. Now what do you think about that?"

I thought about it.

I was still thinking about it when I finally left Headquarters a few minutes before midnight.

Nel Tarey was wearing black silk pajamas when she opened her hotel room door for me. In her bare feet she was even shorter than I'd remembered, the top of her head coming up no higher than the middle of my chest. She looked like a cute miniature of Brigitte Bardot. When she saw it was me, she grabbed my sleeve, yanked me into her room, slammed the door shut behind and whirled to face me.

Her big blue eyes glared at me and her ripe lips pouted. "Where the hell've you been, Jake? I've been calling you and calling you."

"Why? What's up?"

"Me! Way up. In the air. You promised to come back and keep me company from time to time. I'm getting nervous being penned up in this room all by myself."

"Take it easy," I soothed her, patting her softly rounded behind under the black silk.

The TV set in one corner of the room was tuned to a late movie. An easy chair was turned around to face the TV screen. There were three opened beer cans on the rug beside the chair, and four unopened ones on top of the TV set.

She saw me looking at the beer cans and nodded. "That's what happens to me when I get nervous, all charged up and no way to let off steam. I drink beer. And I shouldn't. It's bad for my figure."

I took a long, lingering look at the figure she was talking about. "Hasn't done any damage so far."

Nel grinned and blushed at the same time. "Stop looking at me like I'm something to eat," she said, not sounding like she really minded. "You've been doing that since the first moment I met you."

I grinned back at her. "Doesn't every man you meet?"

She sighed. "It's hard to get used to." She glanced at the four unopened cans atop the TV set. "Do you like beer?"

I nodded. "I could use some."

I watched her walk to the TV set. The unhampered movement of her body in those pajamas was sheer delight to watch. Under the influence of her rampant sex appeal I felt myself relaxing for the first time that night. She punched holes in two of the cans with an opener, switched off the TV set.

"What were you watching?" I asked her as she handed me my beer can.

"A detective movie. Not very exciting." She climbed onto the wide bed and sat in the middle of it with her legs crossed under her. I sat on the edge of the bed and took a long cool swallow of beer from the can in my hand.

Nel Tarey set her beer can on the bed beside her. "Speaking of detective movies, what've you been doing?"

I took another long swig of beer. Then I told her, watching her. She registered a lot of shock, but nothing else that I could detect.

"How awful!" she whispered, staring at me. "You must feel terrible."

"It wasn't fun," I admitted.

"But what is it all about, Jake?"

"Damned if I know. It'd help if you'd remember something that'd give us a hint about what kind of trouble Lewis had gotten himself into."

"There's nothing to remember," Nel insisted. "If there was, it would have come to me by now."

We sat there a while just looking at each other and drinking our beers. Then I told her about the two-way mirror in Angela Hart's apartment, watching her to see if it meant anything to her.

She just looked puzzled. Which made two of us. I finished the beer in my can. The beer added to the soothing effect she was having on me. My tight-wound nerves were coming all uncoiled.

I held up my empty can. "More?"

She gave me a lazy, thoughtful look, then nodded. "Hold it." She chug-a-lugged the rest of her beer. I took the two cans and set them beside the three she'd finished before I showed up. Punching holes in two more, I went back to the bed with them. We sat and drank and didn't say much. I was through trying to work things out for the night. Seeming to sense my mood, she asked no questions.

I was just finishing my second beer when Nel suddenly yawned and stretched prettily, the black silk drawn taut across her breasts. Her eyelids got a heavy look.

"Better get that look out of your eyes," she whispered throatily. "Won't do you a bit of good, Jake. That was my fifth can of beer. I'm all unwound."

"Me too," I told her. "What's bad about unwinding?"

"I unwind all the way." She grinned teasingly. "Maybe I should have warned you. That's something else beer does to me. Makes me sleepy. I'll conk out in a few minutes." She slid off the bed and gazed at me. "Time for you to say goodnight, Jake. Next time come earlier."

I stood up slowly, reluctantly. "Just when I was beginning to relax," I said, letting a suggestion creep into my voice.

She shook her head, sleepily. "Uh-uh," she said, with soft determination. "I don't know you that well yet. A girl's got to have some rules."

I guess I looked sad. She murmured huskily, "Poor Jake," and reached her hands up to my cheeks. Her waist was small and pliant in the grip of my hands. She came against me instantly, her head tipping back, lips parting for a kiss. I bent and fastened my mouth on hers. She kissed with a surprising quality of wantonness. I let my hands slide up to the cushiony soft fullness of her young breasts.

She let me fondle her for a few moments, then tore her mouth from mine and pushed me firmly away from her. "That's all, brother," she panted. "Goodnight." She had a drugged look.

"That's a hell of a way to say goodnight."

She grinned impishly. "How else'll I get to know you better?"

She opened the door, patted my cheek, and gave me another firm "Goodnight."

It was almost two in the morning when the cab dropped me off at my place. I went up to my apartment, got into my pajamas, and took a bottle of rye to bed with me. It was a lousy substitute. But I was wearier than I'd thought, and it didn't take much of the stuff to knock me out.

Some mornings, if nothing disturbs me, I can stay unconscious till I've soaked up twelve hours' sleep. But that morning seven hours was more than I could take. I was wide awake at nine A.M. and I woke up tense.

I went into the kitchenette and brewed my coffee strong, drank three cups with a buttered roll and called it breakfast. Still in my pajamas, I phoned Homicide. I didn't expect Lieutenant Sellers to still be in. He was, though.

"Had a good sleep?" he demanded nastily as a salutation.

"I slept."

"Grand for you, shamus. One of these days I'm

gonna wise up and quit the force. Get myself a private eye license and live the good life too."

"I've got troubles too," I told him. "Someday I'll tell you about them. When you run out of breath complaining about your own troubles."

"I've been up all night with this lousy case," he said, ignoring me. "And you've been sleeping."

"Getting anywhere?" I asked him.

"Nowhere. Like a mouse in a maze. I'm so dead now I wouldn't recognize a clue if it climbed on my shoulder and slapped me in the nose."

"Find out who those two heavies were working for?"

"Nope. All anybody knows is they've been hanging out together the past week or so. Nobody knows who's been paying for their beer. Anyway, nobody's telling."

"How about Angela Hart's friends?"

"She was a loner. No girl friends. She didn't like girls."

"How about men? She liked men."

"And they liked her," Sellers said. "A lot of 'em. We've been checking them out. Can't hang it on any of them. And none of them knows anything that helps."

"Steve Canby, the fight manager, was one of her men," I told him.

"We know. He was throwing a party for the sports writers in the Oran Club last night while Angela and those two hoods were getting themselves killed. And he doesn't know anything, either. Nothing that helps."

"You've had a busy night."

"While you've been sleeping. Now you've had your rest, whyn't you go out and find out what's going on for me? I'm so tired now I can't . . ."

I told him goodbye and hung up.

After I'd dressed, I went out and took a cab to where I'd left my Chevy. There was a ticket for illegal parking under the windshield wiper. I pocketed the ticket and went in search of the nearest gas station. I bought a can of gas, poured it in the tank and drove back to the gas station to have the tank filled. Then I drove to my office in the Times Square area, left the Chevy in a parking lot, and strode the block to my building.

There was a small pile of mail on the desk in the tiny outer office which I always left unlocked. I unlocked the inner door and carried the mail into my inner office, dumped it on my desk there. I turned on the air conditioner, sat down behind my desk and opened the mail. There were bills, advertisements, and a check from an insurance company for a job I'd done for them two weeks before.

My answering service had a message for me to call the adjuster at the same insurance company. I phoned him. He had another small job for me, checking on a gypsy trucker who'd been having too many accidents with his trucks.

I told him to hang on, got out my bank book, and looked at the balance in it. There was enough. I told the insurance adjuster that I was too busy at the moment to handle the job for him.

After I'd hung up, I thought about why I'd said that. No good reason. Except that I felt all wrapped up in a problem that was none of my making, and there was a restless, thrusting need in me to dig into it and make sense of it.

I phoned a friend on the rewrite staff at the *Daily News*. After talking to him I made out a check to the Traffic Bureau, enclosed it in an envelope with my parking ticket, put the check from the insurance company into another envelope addressed to my bank, together with a deposit slip. Then I got my extra gun, a .38 Police Special, out of my desk and strapped it on under my arm and left my office. Dropping the stamped envelopes into the corner mailbox, I got my

Chevy and drove across town to the *Daily News* building.

When it comes to the gorier side of New York life, the morgue files of the *Daily News* are the most complete in the city. But the folder on the Roland Miller murder was pretty thin. My friend let me use his desk in the city room to go through the clippings while he went in search of the reporter who'd handled the story.

There wasn't anything in the newspaper clippings that Lieutenant Sellers hadn't told me, except for the address of Miller's firm, Roland Miller Creations, and some photographs of Miller. He'd been a tall, solidly built man in his late forties, with a handsome, sharply confident face. I studied his face for a while, thinking of him and Angela Hart, until my rewrite friend came back with Ray Fallon, the reporter who'd been on the Miller story.

Ray Fallon was an undersized, scrawny man in an ill-fitting summer suit. He looked to be about fifty, and a lot of whiskey had gotten to his face, aging it more than his half-century. But not his eyes. They were the eyes of an overly bright sixteen-year-old.

His eyes fastened on me eagerly as he perched on the edge of the desk, pushing aside the clippings to make room for his meager buttocks. "Something new cooking on the Roland Miller kill?"

"Maybe," I told him. "If you've got any information that helps, I might be able to stir something up. If I do, you get a beat on it."

"Fair enough," Fallon agreed. "What do you want to know?" He tapped the clippings with his nicotine-stained fingertips. "You've already gone through these."

"I want whatever you know that *didn't* get in the papers."

Fallon grinned wolfishly. "Like who did it?"

"Do you know?"

MARVIN ALBERT 69

"Uh-uh. But if you're asking about motive, there's always the wife."

"Jealousy?"

"Maybe. I don't think so. I met her. Nora Miller. Good-looking dish. But she didn't seem hot-blooded enough for a jealous rage. For her, I'd say there was a motive that fitted better."

"Like what?"

"Everything Roland Miller had went to his wife after he got killed. His business, money and a juicy chunk of life insurance. And the house and estate he left her out on the North Shore are worth a small fortune, if she'd wanted to sell. Only she didn't have to sell them, with everything else he left her. She still lives out there, just her and the servants."

"How'd Nora Miller take her husband's death?"

"She didn't act too broken up about it."

"The way you see it, Miller's death was a windfall for her?"

Fallon nodded. "Her and her brother. Fred Usher. He's running her dead husband's business for her, now. Maybe neither of them did the murder, or had anything to do with it. But they sure benefited from it. Nora and Fred Usher come from a family that used to be big in the garment industry. But their father went broke and killed himself. Until Nora married Roland Miller, she and her brother were living off a little second-hand clothing store Fred Usher ran down on the lower East Side."

"That means there was somebody else with a motive for killing Roland Miller," I said. "Nora's brother, Fred."

"Sure. More motive than you think. Because even after Nora married Miller four years ago, Fred Usher went on running that second-hand store. I don't know why. But he did."

"Maybe Roland Miller and Fred Usher didn't get along," I suggested. "A lot of in-laws don't."

"Could be. Anyway, Fred Usher stuck to that store of his until Miller got killed. Then he became manager of Miller's firm. And it's a real prosperous firm."

"The cops knew all this, of course."

"Sure they did," Fallon said. "And they dug into it, too. But both Nora and her brother were visiting out-of-town relatives the night Roland Miller got knocked off. So there you are."

"Convenient for them."

"Real. But Nora and Fred Usher have influential contacts, from their father's good days. And once Miller was dead, Nora was a wealthy citizen in her own right. So the cops dropped that angle of the case pretty quick. They'd have dropped it anyway, because there just wasn't any solid evidence against Nora and Fred Usher to hang their suspicions on."

"How about you?" I asked Fallon. "Did you dig into that angle any further?"

Fallon shook his head. "I started to. I went out to the North Shore and started asking around about Nora and Roland Miller. But they've got cops out there that're really rough on anybody that bothers their solid citizens, like Nora Miller. And I'm brittle. I break too easy. So I figured to hell with it."

"You don't look to me like you'd scare off something that easy."

"Not if I was on something that looked like it was really going to lead me somewhere. But I wasn't."

I thanked him, got Nora Miller's address, and left the *Daily News* Building.

Outside, I got into my car, took the bridge across the East River to Long Island, and headed for the North Shore residence of Roland Miller's widow.

EIGHT

After miles of highway I cut into an old country road that twisted and climbed its way through heavily-wooded hills, sighting an occasional big farmhouse in the snug valleys. The road emerged onto a thin strip of high land with the waters of the Sound on either side of it. I tooled the Chevy along that strip for a mile before the land widened again and the road curved its way between alternate patches of thick forest and well-tended estates. Here, I caught glimpses through the trees of the great Victorian mansions and bastard-Norman castles and Spanish-Moroccan villas that served now as fortresses for the old-rich who still lived in them. Nora Miller's house wasn't like those. Roland Miller had been new-rich.

I cut off the road into a wide driveway that plunged through a pine forest for half a mile. It suddenly emerged on the flat top of a wide hill behind a handsome, long and low modern house built of cypress, stone and glass, with an uninterrupted view of a private pebbly beach and the water below.

As I parked my Chevy between a canary-yellow Cadillac and a fire-engine-red Jaguar, a Chinese houseboy came out of one of the rear doors of the building.

"Can I help you, sir?" he asked. He didn't sound any less polite because my Chevy wasn't that year's model.

"Mrs. Miller can," I told him.

"Mrs. Miller is down at the beach. Whom shall I say is . . ."

My thanks cut him short. I went around him and around the side of the building fast enough to leave him behind.

There was a huge red rubber mat spread on the

beach below, near the edge of the sun-dazzled water. There were a man and a woman stretched out on the mat, both in bathing suits that showed lots of deeply tanned skin. The woman was lazily rubbing suntan oil on the man's back.

I went down the steps cut into the stone of the hill. When my shoes crunched on the pebbles near them they both sat up, turning to look at me.

Nora Miller was a dark-haired woman in her late thirties, with a rather exotic face spoiled by a too-tight mouth. Her body, displayed by a black bikini straining at her breasts and hips, had a deep, even tan.

The guy with her was about eight years younger, a gorgeous hunk of man with weight-lifter's muscles and a striking resemblance to Cary Grant. I'll admit that wasn't a decent reason for disliking him on sight.

I envied them their bathing suits. The confinement of my jacket and the weight of the gun under my arm were oppressive under the blazing noon sun. My shirt was sticky against the skin of my back. I wiped my damp palms on my trousers and said, "Mrs. Miller?"

"Yes?"

"My name's Barrow. I'm a detective, from Manhattan. I have to ask you some questions about Angela Hart."

Nora Miller looked puzzled. "Who?"

"Angela Hart. You remember her. Your late husband was keeping her when he got himself murdered."

Nora Miller's mouth got tighter, thinner. "Oh. What about her?"

"You know why I'm here. She's dead. Murdered."

Nora Miller got to her feet, staring at me. I could detect nothing but surprise and curiosity in her face. Muscle boy stood up beside her, looking vaguely protective.

"So she's dead," Nora Miller said harshly. "Good for her."

"You make it sound like you didn't know about it till now."

"How would I?"

"It was in the papers this morning."

"I haven't seen today's papers."

"That's convenient," I said. "It happened last night. Where were you last night?"

She sucked in a deep, shocked breath. "Are . . . are you accusing *me?*"

"I'm asking you."

For a second she looked frightened, then indignant. "You have a hell of a nerve, coming here and . . ."

Muscle boy laid a thick hand on her bare shoulders. "Just a minute, Nora." He eyed me wisely. "Let's see your identification."

I stared back at him. "And who're you?"

"Ben Massey," he said. "But it's you I'm . . ."

"You live here?"

It confused him momentarily. "What? . . . No. I'm just visiting Mrs. . . ." He caught himself, his eyes narrowing. "You claim to be a cop. You're supposed to show proof." He dropped his hand from her shoulder and took a threatening step toward me.

"I said I was a detective," I corrected him. I took out my wallet, flipped it open.

He took it from my hand, looked at the photostat of my license. He sneered at it, tossed the wallet back at me. I caught it with both hands.

"You don't have to talk to him," Ben Massey told Nora Miller. "He's just a private peeper."

I slipped the wallet back in my pocket. "You don't have to talk to me," I admitted. "But you should unless you've got something to hide."

Nora Miller glared at me. "What is this? Some kind of blackmail attempt? If it is, I'm warning you I won't . . ."

"All I want is some information. There's been two murders in the past few days. Angela Hart, and a man named Ernest Lewis. Did you know him?"

Nora Miller shook her head. "No."

I looked at Ben Massey. "How about you?"

"Never heard of him."

"How about Angela Hart? Know her?"

"Of course not."

"Why *of course?*"

Massey frowned and licked his lips briefly. "I just meant I never knew her. Why would I have?"

I looked back at Nora Miller. "But *you* did know her. Right?"

"After Roland died, I heard about her."

"You knew before that," I ventured. I was beginning to get sore about having made the trip all the way out there only to run into a pair like this. "You knew she was your husband's mistress. Maybe you were even getting afraid of losing him to her?"

She sucked in another deep breath that was almost reward enough for me. "Get out of here," she hissed through her teeth. "Get out or I'll . . ."

"Of course," I snapped, "you and your brother had dandy alibis all set up for the night your husband got it. But that doesn't mean anything. You could have hired someone to do the job while you were off somewhere else. Like it was done with Angela Hart last night."

I was just trying to scare her into giving me some answers. It scared her just fine. But not into any answers. She gasped and looked to Ben Massey for protection.

Massey did what her look demanded. His knees bent a little and his hands squeezed into fists. He moved in and swung at me. His muscles were highly decorative but slow. His fist might have been forcing its way through molasses for all the speed it achieved. I caught his fist like a baseball with both hands. The thrust of my thumbs into the backs of his knuckles twisted his hand, locking his wrist, elbow and shoulder, and turning his arm into a rigid lever. I increased the pressure of my thumbs just enough to flip him face down on the pebbles of the beach.

Nora Miller had sprinted away from us and was racing up the stone steps toward the house above. I let go of Ben Massey and started after her.

Massey came up off the pebbles and locked his arms around my neck. I jammed my elbow backward against his middle. His muscles there were ungiving as interlocked boards. He didn't even grunt. He got a knee against my back. His arms dragged me backward over it. I kicked the hard heel of my shoe against his bare shin.

He yelled, "Ow!" and let go of me and sat down hard on the pebbles.

I spun around and looked down at him sitting there. "You can cut it out now. Your audience is gone."

He got up slowly, measuring the distance between us.

"Don't," I warned him.

He threw a punch at me, faster than before. But I was expecting it. I dodged and backed away from him. "You've already proved you're brave and tough. I'm willing to call it quits if you are."

The determination on his movie-star face just got tighter. He came on after me and swung again.

By then I knew there was no use arguing further with him. I slipped inside his punch and slammed my right against the point of his chin. It was one of those blows that landed just right; I felt the shock run up my arm from my bruised knuckles to my shoulder. His head snapped back and then lolled forward. His eyes closed. He fell asleep on the way down.

I stood over him, breathing hard, sore at myself for the clumsy way I'd handled myself with Massey and Nora Miller. Massey lay on his back, his handsome face turned up to the sun. His breathing was heavy but regular. I turned away from him and trudged across the beach and slowly climbed the stone steps to the house.

I opened the first door I came to, entered a long screened sundeck with cypress paneling and Danish modern furniture. The room was divided off from a big, gleaming kitchen by a low serving counter with a white marble top. Nora Miller was there talking into a phone. As I entered, she hung up and turned angrily to face me.

"That was the police I just called," she informed me. "You'd better get out while you still can."

"I've got nothing to hide from the police," I told her as I crossed the sundeck. "Have you?"

"Don't come near me!" she yelled.

I halted at the serving counter. "Now listen, Mrs. Miller. You've got no reason to act like this. All I want . . ."

"What did you do to Ben?"

"He's taking a nap." I walked around the end of the counter.

There was a swinging door in the kitchen, leading deeper into the house. The door swung open and the Chinese houseman came through it, carrying a .22 rifle.

"Please," he begged, aiming the rifle at me. "Stand still."

I stood still. There is nothing more dangerous than a frightened man with a gun in his hands.

"If you've hurt Ben . . ." Nora Miller warned me. Her concern for Massey was the first genuine emotion she'd displayed in my presence.

"You can make him an ice-pack. He'll wake up with a headache."

"You'll be sorry," she promised me, with nasty certainty.

The cops arrived inside four minutes. Two of them. They were local township cops in summer tans and wide-brimmed ranger hats. Both were young and big and heavily muscled. One had the freckled, pug-nosed face of a red-haired Irishman and the other's face was dark and hawk-nosed.

The hawk-nosed one waved a .38 revolver at me and told the others, "Looks like he's wearing a gun, Mike. Get it."

Mike didn't appear to appreciate being ordered around. But he nodded and came at me empty-handed, got the gun from my shoulder holster and stepped back after patting my pockets for further weapons.

Hawk-nose took the gun from Mike and slipped it inside the front of his belt. He holstered his own revolver and looked at Nora Miller. "This the guy trying to shake you down, Mrs. Miller?"

Somehow, with them in the room, her bikini did less than before to prevent her from looking totally naked. But she didn't seem to care. She looked directly into Hawk-nose's eyes and nodded. "Yes."

"That just isn't so," I said. "I'm a private detective."

"Yeah? So what?"

"So I'm not a blackmailer. I came here to ask Mrs. Miller some questions about a woman who was murdered last night in the city. A woman who knew her husband. She didn't have to answer my questions, but I had a right to ask them."

"He threatened me!" Nora Miller shouted. "He beat up a guest of mine and . . ."

"It's the other way around," I said. "Her guest tried to beat me up. I protected myself."

"Are you calling Mrs. Miller a liar?" Hawk-nose asked mildly.

"That's right."

He backhanded me across the face. He didn't seem to put much effort behind it, but it was hard enough to knock me sideways against the serving counter.

Hawk-nose grinned and watched me, waiting for my anger to send me against him. I stayed where I was, feeling the burning of my cheek where he'd hit me. I was angry, but not out of control. You don't attack a cop. Not if you have a private detective's license and want to keep it.

"Ridge," the other cop snapped, "you'd better take it easy."

"Who says?" Ridge demanded.

"Me."

"Okay. You've said it. Now cuff him. Behind."

Mike hesitated, not liking it. He glanced at Nora Miller. "Are you preferring charges against this man, Mrs. Miller? For attempted blackmail?"

It frightened her a little. She shook her head quickly. "No. I don't want to be involved in anything like that. I . . ." She looked at the hawk-nosed cop. "I just don't want him to bother me anymore."

"Don't worry," he told her, almost tenderly. His eyes roamed her ripe flesh. "I'll see he don't come back here again."

Her smile of thanks warmed him. "I appreciate that, Ridge," she told him softly.

I took a deep breath, told the two cops, "Before this goes any further, call Lieutenant Sellers at Homicide in Manhattan. He'll vouch for me. I'm sort of working for him on this."

Ridge sneered at me. "Listen, creep, I don't need any big deal city cop to tell me what to do with you."

"Ridge," Mike said, hesitantly, "maybe you'd better . . ."

"Shut up and put the cuffs on him," Ridge growled.

Mike's face stiffened with anger. But he got the handcuffs off his belt and came over to me.

"Behind his back," Ridge snapped.

Mike turned me around and cuffed my wrists together behind me.

Ridge motioned to me. "Okay, creep. Let's go." Nora Miller watched smugly as they marched me out of her house.

There was a black township police car parked behind my Chevy, the red light on its roof revolving and blinking, like a miniature lighthouse beacon. We stopped beside it.

"You go on with the prowl car," Ridge told Mike. "I'm taking the private creep here in his own heap."

"Where you figure on taking him?" Mike asked, uncertainly.

"To the station."

"Ferguson ain't there. It's his day off."

"I know that. So what?"

"We better phone his house, ask him about it first."

"What for?"

Mike looked defensive. "Well, after all . . . Ferguson is the Chief."

"No need to bother him with this. I ain't gonna book this boy. Just have a little talk with him."

Mike frowned and chewed his lip. "I don't know, Ridge . . ."

"I *do* know," Ridge snapped. "One a these days I'll be the Chief of Police around here. You want to stay in my good book, just blow and let me take care of this my way."

Mike glanced at me, still frowning.

I tried desperately to reverse the directions things were headed in. "All it'll cost you is one phone call to the city to check on my side of this."

"Nobody cares about your side of it," Ridge informed me flatly. "Mrs. Miller's a respected citizen around here. Guys that come in here bothering our respected citizens gotta learn not to come back and try it again." He turned back to Mike and said with finality, "Be seeing you, Mike."

Mike glanced at me again, shrugged, and went to the police car. After he drove away, Ridge opened the side door of my car and motioned for me to get in.

I knew what he was taking me to, and I was in no hurry to get there. "Listen," I argued, "stop thinking with your muscles and let's make some sense. I . . ."

He backhanded me again. I was ready for it, and I rolled with it, enough so it only stung me. But I didn't enjoy it. I got into the front seat of my car, moving awkwardly because of my wrists being handcuffed behind me. Ridge slammed the door and walked around the car to the other side, got in behind the steering wheel. He drove away without saying another word or looking at me again, just whistling through his teeth softly and watching the road ahead, anticipation making his hawk-nosed face look almost cheerful.

The police station was a one-storey brick building behind town hall near the shopping section in the center of the village. Ridge marched me into a wide clean office containing several desks empty except for a single uniformed township cop at the phone switchboard. He glanced at us curiously as we went through the office and out through another door. Ridge pushed me ahead of him down a short, narrow corridor to a bank of three barred cells, all of them empty.

The door of one of the cells was open. A skinny, bald janitor was inside it, mopping the floor. He grinned at the sight of us, showing a few yellowed teeth with a lot of spaces between them.

"Thanks for the company, Ridge," he rasped. "It was getting damn lonely around here."

"He ain't staying long," Ridge told him. He looked at me and smiled. "Just till I get tired. I don't tire very quick, though." He looked at the janitor again. "Go out and have a few beers. Have 'em slow."

"Hell, do I got to miss the fun again?"

"Scram," Ridge warned him.

"I won't squeal on you, Ridge. You know that."

"I said scram!"

The janitor scrammed.

When he was gone, Ridge shoved me into the open cell. He came in behind me, nodded at the bunk chained to the brick wall. "Sit down, creep."

I sat down on the edge of the bunk, holding myself taut, ready to move whenever he did. I knew it wasn't going to save me from anything, in the long run. But nobody's geared to just sit and take it.

He reached inside my jacket and took out my wallet. I watched him open it and look at my license. "Jacob Barrow," he read from it. He looked over it at me. "Looks legal. A private eye. Some of you guys are supposed to be real tough. You one of the tough ones?"

"You can still phone the city about me," I told him. My voice sounded shaky. I clamped my teeth together to stop myself from saying anymore. He tossed my wallet on the bunk beside me and smiled down at me. I hated him with an intensity that shook me. I knew nothing I could say was going to stop him. The sick sadism of the man showed plainly in his face.

"Yeah," he whispered happily, "you are one of the tough ones. You know, the place I used to work before here, we had an air compression tank we used on the tough ones like you. Pumped air into 'em. Takes about ten seconds of that to turn the toughest creep to jelly . . . Only I don't have a compression tank."

He moved faster than I'd expected, in a way I hadn't expected. His hands shot out at my face. One clamped hard over my mouth. The fingers of the other pinched my nostrils shut.

I bucked and twisted like a hooked shark. But I couldn't pull out of his grasp. My wrists yanked uselessly at the steel cuffs behind me as I fought for breath. I tried desperately to get at him with my legs. He fell on top of me with all his weight, pinning me down on the cot, his hands and fingers retaining their brutal grips, keeping air from my tortured, heaving lungs.

My head bloated. Darkness closed around my bulging eyes, darkness ripped by blood-red comets. Knives ripped at the inner linings of my lungs. Dammed-up blood pounded in my ears. The thought flickered briefly far inside the swirling, bloodshot darkness of my dimming brain: If Ridge didn't pull out of the grip of his violent passion soon enough, I would be dead.

NINE

My lungs gulped in fresh air for some time before I realized that I was breathing again. Then the dark swirling fog before my eyes began to shred apart. A hand swept through the dissolving fog and smacked hard against the side of my face.

"Sit up and smile, creep," Ridge's voice rasped at me. "We still got a lot ahead of us. You wouldn't want to miss any of it."

I smelled him before I could see him. His smell was rank, strong. He hadn't smelled that way before.

I sat up slowly on the edge of the bunk, lowering my feet to the stone floor. My head deflated to normal size and my vision cleared. Ridge stood in the middle of the cell, gazing at me like a hungry man viewing a thick, juicy steak.

"That was something, wasn't it?" he murmured. "That always scares hell out of 'em. Trouble is, when it's over it don't leave 'em nothing to remember you by. And I like to be remembered."

He took out a short, wicked-looking blackjack and slapped it into the palm of his left hand. It cracked like the report of a gun.

"I'm an expert with this," he whispered, dragging out the words. "I know how to shatter every bone in your face without knocking you out. I can work on your tendons with it so's it'll be years before your arms and legs work right for you again."

My stomach knotted. "This could be big trouble for you," I told him, as evenly as I could. The wild rage inside me was fighting to break loose. It took all my control to hold it back. "This is a murder investigation you're interfering with."

"Only you ain't a real cop."

"I'm working with one. Lieutenant Sellers of Homicide, in Manhattan. He won't like this."

"Maybe your Lieutenant carries weight in Manhattan. But this ain't Manhattan." Ridge smacked the blackjack hard against one of the cell bars, wanting me to hear the ringing impact of it. I heard it, and winced despite myself. Ridge grinned, pleased. "I'll take my chances. Nobody cares what I do to a cheap private creep like you."

"Why? You've got nothing to gain."

"The hell I ain't. I'll tell you something. We got an old Chief of Police here. Name's Ferguson. He's retiring next year. I'm gonna be the new Chief. Things like this're gonna help me make it. Nora Miller's an important citizen in this township. It's people like her that decide who gets to be anything in this town. I see to it you don't bother her again. She spreads word with the other bigwigs that I'm the boy who knows how to keep the city filth from spreading out here."

"Okay," I told him, struggling to get the words out before my control slipped as it was threatening to any second. "I get your message. I go and don't come back. You don't have to beat it into me."

"Of course you'd say that. Only I like to be sure." He drifted toward me with the blackjack poised ready in his hand. "This'll make it sure."

His smile was pure sick evil. He leaned over me, bringing up the blackjack to begin his job of destruction. I kicked him in the throat.

A hideously strangled scream filtered out of his mouth, thin and faint as a whisper. His eyes bulged and glazed. His face swelled, dark with trapped blood. Blocked choking sounds continued to bubble out of him as his legs buckled and he collapsed forward against my legs, his forehead banging down on my lap. He slid down my legs till his weight was on my feet and ankles.

I turned my head for a fast glance through the open cell door. There was no one in sight in the corridor, and no sounds of alarm. I worked my feet out from under Ridge's stiff weight and went down on my knees beside him. His bulging eyes were open, but nothing in them revealed any human awareness. The tendons of his neck were drawn out taut as piano wires under the bruised skin. The rest of him was rigid as leather-wrapped stone, except for the labored, heaving gasps that were the nearest he could get to breathing.

I turned my back on him and sat on the stone floor of the cell. The handcuffs linking my wrists hindered the job of searching through his pockets. By the time my fingers finally closed around a ring of keys perspiration was rolling down my face. Time was flitting by too fast; at any moment another cop might come through the corridor to the cells and find me at it. I knew too damn well what was going to happen to me if I didn't make it out of there. An hour after Ridge came around all that would be left of me would be one-hundred and eighty pounds of fresh ground hamburger.

Being unable to see what I was doing, the job of trying to fit each key on the ring in turn into the cuff lock took a nerve-plucking amount of time. Behind me, Ridge's labored breathing began to sound more regular. The thought of him coming to before I got loose made my fingers so clumsy in their haste that I dropped the ring of keys on the floor. That meant I had to pick them up and start all over again, not knowing which keys I'd already tested.

Ridge was breathing almost normally, though his eyes still looked as empty as two dusty marbles, when I finally got the cuffs off. Switching around on my knees, I wasted no time rubbing my chafed wrists. I got my .38 out of his belt, slipped it into my shoulder holster, and shoved to my feet. I was out in the corridor a second later. There were two doors leading out of the corridor. One would take me into the outer office where the cop sat at the switchboard. I tried the other door.

It let me out onto a grass-bordered path behind the building. I walked around the building toward the street, knowing that I was walking too fast, but considering it a triumph of will power that I wasn't running. Reaching the pavement alongside the building, I started across it to my parked Chevy.

The jail janitor came out of a saloon across the street.

He stopped dead when he saw me. His mouth popped open. He stared at me, frowning.

I gave him my biggest smile and waved to him. It startled him. He started to smile and raise his arm for an answering wave. But by the time I was behind my steering wheel he'd dropped his hand and was back to frowning. I started the motor, let out the brake, and pulled away from the curb. As I drove off, I looked in the rear-view mirror and saw the janitor crossing the street to the station house. I had to fight myself to keep the speedometer down to thirty miles an hour till I was out of the village. Then I let go and gunned the motor, racing for the nearest highway back to the city.

When I got outside the township limits without being caught, I relaxed a little. But not too much. Ridge had two choices. He could decide to forget the whole thing, or he could send out a call for the state police to pick me up. If he decided on the latter, I was going to

have one hell of a session with the Police Commis-
sioner, trying to justify a violent escape from a law
officer. The odds were that no amount of justification
would save my license. My only hope was that Ridge
was too anxious to become Chief of Police in his township to chance the unpleasant publicity the hearing
would smear on him.

I didn't relax all the way till I got through the Mid-
town Tunnel into Manhattan without being stopped.
If Ridge had sent out a wanted notice on me, the cops
would have been on the lookout for my car at every
exit off Long Island. And if Ridge hadn't done it by
then, he wasn't going to do it.

The relief that flooded me as I tooled the Chevy into
the city traffic left me limp. I knew what my next move
was. But I knew I wasn't going to be in condition for
anything till I'd had a hefty drink, a shower, a change
of clothes and a solid steak dinner inside me. The drink
first, right away. Make it three of them.

TEN

The Seventh Avenue Garment District was jammed
with traffic as usual, and all the curbside space in the
narrow cross streets was lined with solid walls of
parked trucks loading dresses and coats and unloading
material and accessories. I finally left my car in a tiny
parking lot in the west Twenties and walked back
through eight blocks of crowded pavements.

The building was a crazy hybrid. The bottom half
was old and old-fashioned, constructed of stone and
brick, with small conventional windows. On top of this
had recently been added a tall skyscraper extension
made of lots of glass held together with corrugated alu-
minum. The directory in the lobby told me that Roland
Miller Creations took up the seventh, eighth and ninth

floors. I took one of the elevators up to the seventh.

I emerged from the elevator into a big combination lobby and reception room with gleaming gray plastic walls in which were recessed showcases displaying the new line of Roland Miller frocks on lifelike plaster mannequins. The place was crawling with noisy people chattering and laughing and generally having a fine time. Everybody in sight had a drink in hand. Somewhere a small band was beating out dance tunes against the din of voices. I'd walked in on some kind of company party.

It was a break. I didn't have to explain myself or make a formal point of the questions I wanted to ask. I drifted in through the partying crowd, unchallenged. Nobody knew me, but nobody cared. As I circulated, I noticed that the people around me divided into two distinct types. There were middle-aged men and women. And there were good-looking young men and very pretty girls. When I pushed my way into a long, wide showroom, where a four-man band was working away on a platform at one end, I saw that the middle-aged men danced with the pretty girls and the middle-aged women were dancing with the good-looking boys. A sensible arrangement.

I spotted the tables where drinks and snacks were being served up across the showroom to my right, and started working my way toward it. A tall, lovely creature in a pale green cocktail dress and red shoes bumped into me. Some of the highball she was carrying slopped out of the tall glass. We both jumped backward. The liquid splashed to the floor between us.

She put her free hand to her wide mouth and giggled, her green eyes rounding at me, and blurted, "Oops!"

"Oops, yourself," I said, smiling at her. She was worth a smile. She had more than her share of healthy good looks, and an athletic figure built for trouble. The kind of trouble no man would mind getting into.

"I guess I'm getting drunk," she said, and giggled again.

"You're doing just fine," I assured her.

"You a buyer?" she asked me, drifting close, a little unsteady on her pins.

"Uh-huh."

"Where's your drink then? You're supposed to be drinking."

"And what're *you* supposed to be doing?"

"Me? I'm one of the models here. I'm supposed to see to it you out-of-town buyers are having fun."

"That's just dandy for us men," I told her. "But how about the women buyers?"

She winked at me. "We got some real hot-looking salesmen. Hey, you sure you're a buyer?"

"Sure."

"You don't look like a buyer," she said, like she didn't really care. "My name's Penny. What's yours?"

"Jake."

"Shake, Jake." She started to reach out her hand, then realized she was holding the highball glass in it. She handed it to me. "Here. You take it. You're supposed to be drinking. I'm already high. I get much higher and old man Usher'll get sore."

I took the highball from her. "Where is Fred Usher?"

She shrugged. "Who knows? Who cares? The straight-laced so-'n-so."

A big, paunchy man with a florid face came up behind Penny, grabbed her, and whirled her around to face him. "Hi ya, honey bunch," he growled, grinning at her. "Wanna dance?"

She melted automatically into his embrace. As he danced off with her through the crowd, she winked back at me over his shoulder.

I tasted the drink in the glass she'd given me. It was too sweet for my taste. I carried it across the room to the serving tables, set it down next to a tray of those tiny party sandwiches. There were four white-jacketed waiters behind the tables, working like madmen to keep up with the general thirst. It took me a good four minutes to get my order in. I asked for rye and got it— a tumbler filled to the brim with it, plus a couple ice-cubes. Beside me, a baldheaded buyer in a rumpled suit ordered Scotch and got it the same way, a tumblerful.

We turned away from the tables together, eying our glasses dubiously.

"Well," the man beside me muttered, "at least Usher ain't stingy with his liquor. Here's looking at you."

We clicked glasses. He took a mighty gulp of his drink. I matched him. The mouthful of straight rye hit my insides and lighted a bonfire.

"Nice party," I ventured.

"They used to be better," he growled. "When Rollie Miller threw a party . . . Wow! This is nothing. This Usher may be okay as a businessman. But when it comes to throwing parties, Miller really was in there. What a crazy guy that Miller was, eh?"

I nodded meaninglessly and we matched drinks again. "I haven't seen Fred Usher yet," I said. "Have you?"

"Nah. He probably went home right after this started. Parties ain't his line. A real stick-in-the-mud. You done anything with him yet?"

"Not yet."

"I have. He's okay, I guess. Straight enough. Honest and all. But old Rollie Miller . . . there was a guy knew how to enjoy life, right?"

"This is my first time to New York," I told him. "I never met Roland Miller. What was he like?"

"Like? He . . ."

But just then a tall, slinky blonde in an evening gown with a V-neckline that plunged all the way down to there strutted past. The eyes of the man beside me went with her, and he followed his eyes, without a word of goodbye. I didn't blame him.

I stood there a while alone, drinking and looking around. By the time I finished my glass of rye I was getting more and more interested in some of the girls in sight, and less and less concerned with what I'd come there for. I wanted a refill, but it was getting more crowded near the tables, the thirsty customers lining up three deep. So I walked around behind the tables and picked up one of the opened bottles of rye from the floor. The rushing, perspiring waiters didn't even notice.

Refilling my glass, I wandered toward one of the inner doorways with the bottle in one hand, my glass in the other, with the notion of locating Fred Usher somewhere. The notion was pretty vague. The liquor I'd already consumed was beginning to get a grip on me. When I located my old friend Penny, instead of Usher, I shifted notions with no effort.

She maneuvered her way through the crowd toward me, an empty glass in her hand. "You're the smartest man in this joint," she said by way of greeting as she reached me by the wall. She held out her empty glass.

I tipped the bottle and poured her glass full. "Drink up, Penny."

She did. As though it were water.

"Hey," she said, "you aren't drinking. You're supposed to be drinking, too." Her voice was getting a slurred, thick-tongued sound to it.

I drank. Then I refilled our glasses from the bottle.

"You're a real pal, Jake. Got a last name?"

"Barrow. How about you?"

"Banks," she said, and looked at me.

"Penny Banks. Cute."

"I made it up," she told me, with drunk seriousness. "So people'd remember me."

I looked her up and down, slowly and thoroughly.

"You didn't have to," I told her. "There's so much else about you that's memorable."

She giggled and waggled a finger at me. "Oh, what naughty thoughts you're thinking!"

"Nothing thought, nothing ventured," I told her, and knew by the way my voice reverberated in my eardrums that I was getting high. "And nothing ventured . . ."

"You never know," she said, agreeably. "You're pretty cute yourself. You're not very pretty. But you're cute, anyway."

"Thanks a bunch."

We leaned against the wall together, grinning at each other.

"Nice party," I ventured again.

"Too tame," she said. "When Roland Miller was running things, those were real parties in those days. Wild? Wow!"

"You knew Miller?"

"Knew him?" she slurred, and winked at me. "You bet I knew him."

My interest in Penny Banks quickened. "What was he like?"

"A slob," Penny said, without rancor. "But a rich slob. He knew how to treat a gal right. And like I said, when he tossed a party . . . Didn't you ever get to any of 'em?"

"Nope."

"Boy what *you* missed!"

"If you were there, I agree."

"I like you," she whispered, throatily. "Like you, like you. . . ." She turned her head slowly and looked around at the crowd swirling about us. I *think* the crowd was swirling. Maybe it was me.

"This is a drag," Penny said. "A real drag. C'mon." She grabbed my wrist and led me out of the room, into a narrow corridor. There she stopped and turned to face me, her body against mine. "Let's go be alone and drink and things and to hell with Fred Usher's cube party. Okay?"

"Okay with me," I told her.

She led me through the models' dressing room, into another corridor, to a flight of stairs leading upward to the next floor. At the foot of the stairs she halted. "I don't know," she murmured, eying the stairs. "The way I feel, I'm not going to make it all the way up there."

"Sure you will," I assured her. "You go first. I'll push."

It sounded like a good idea. She started up the steps and I followed, putting my hands against her rear end and pushing. It *was* a good idea. She wasn't wearing any girdle.

By the time we reached the top, we were both laughing like hysterical idiots. The next thing I knew, she had wrapped her arms around me and was mashing her lips against mine. I wrapped my arms around her and mashed back. Her hips began moving in a slow, knowing way against me. As I mentioned, she wasn't wearing any girdle. Neither was I.

When we finally came out of the clinch she was grinning at me crookedly. "Yum-yum," she murmured, and dragged me down an empty dim-lighted corridor, into a small office. She closed and locked the door behind us, and leered at me. "Now," she drawled, "I have you in my power."

We stood there a moment grinning at each other.

"I'm high as a kite," she told me happily. "How about you?"

"Flying."

"Grand! . . . You know what? It's too damn hot in here for this lousy dress." She turned her back to me, raising her hands behind her head to hold her hair up out of the way. "Unbutton, please."

I went to work on the line of buttons down the back of her dress. My fingers felt swollen to the size of bananas. But somehow I got it done. When I finished with the lowest button, she shrugged her shoulders out of the dress and let it fall to a piled circle around her ankles.

She stepped out of the circle and turned to face me again, wearing just her high-heeled red shoes, pale green sheer nylons, and a pale green nylon slip. She wasn't wearing anything at all under the slip. Her breasts were high and conical, the rest of her. . . .

"Now I feel cooler," she announced.

"Now I feel warmer," I said.

She giggled and plastered herself against me and we went into a long kiss that left my head reeling and the rest of me throbbing. There was a leather couch against one wall. Somehow, we made our way to it and sat down in it. Her face had a blurred look to it that matched the way I felt.

She held out her glass and I poured it full again.

"How about you?" she demanded.

I hesitated. My back teeth were already afloat.

"Don't be a party pooper!" she snapped.

I didn't want her getting sore at me, so I filled my glass and set the bottle down on the floor.

"Boy," she blurted, between gulps, "if old prune-face Usher could see us now!"

"What would he do?"

"Fire me. That's what he'd do . . . I don't care. There're other jobs. Aren't many of us old gals left here anyway. Freddie Usher doesn't like our type."

"Old girls?"

"The ones Rollie Miller hired. Miller knew what he was doing when *he* picked a model to work for *him*. He never hired a girl that didn't look cooperative, if you know what I mean."

I leered at her. She leered back. "I'm *real* cooperative," she whispered. "Only you aren't trying very hard to find that out. How come?"

"You just wait," I promised her.

"Maybe you haven't had enough to drink."

Her frown made me take another slug of the rye. I was having a battle trying to slow the rocking of my brain.

"I used to know one girl that worked here," I said. My voice sounded blurry, but I concentrated and managed to get out the rest of it. "Name of Angela Hart. Know her?"

Penny made a nasty face. "I knew her all right. Matter've fact, I was sort of Roland Miller's girl . . . one of his girls . . . before that Hart bitch came to work as a model here."

"She snatched Miller away from you?"

Penny nodded solemnly. "He fell for her like a ton. Didn't see me for dust after that."

"He must've been blind. Or nuts. Or both."

Penny rewarded me with another of her juicy, suction kisses.

"Any guy that'd drop a girl who kisses like you do . . ." I gasped.

"I don't know," Penny mused, shaking her head drunkenly. "Maybe Angy Hart had something extra. She must've. 'Cause she didn't work here long. First thing you know, Miller had her set up in a real lush apartment, with the rent all paid and a new mink . . . The works."

"You must've been pretty sore about it. Sore at him."

"Nah. Not really. That was the kind've guy he was. What the hell . . . Pour me another, will you?"

I poured her another. "Sore at Angela Hart, then?" I suggested.

"Not for long. We all knew . . . me and the other girls . . . that it wouldn't last long for her. Miller liked variety, see? And sure enough, a few weeks after he started shacking up with the Hart dame, he was back to making passes at another new girl he'd just hired."

Despite my condition, it registered on me. "And he dropped Angela Hart?"

"Would've . . . eventually. Bet on it. But he never got the chance, though. Got himself killed in an alley. Some mugger got too rough, I guess . . . Next thing we knew, Fred Usher's the new boss around here. What a come-down!"

"Usher's not like Miller was?"

Penny shook her head. "You kidding? Usher's completely different. Opposite. Not a single pass at any of us girls, so far. He's strictly business . . ."

She turned her head suddenly and glared drunkenly at me. "How about *you*? You strictly business, too? 'Cause I didn't come up here just to yak."

"I had something else in mind, too," I assured her. "But about . . ."

"To hell with all this gab," she growled, cutting me off. She downed the rest of her liquor, dropped the glass on the floor and swayed to her feet. She planted her feet apart, put her hands on her hips, and grinned down at me. "Like?" she cooed.

"Uh-huh. Now about . . ."

"It's too damn hot for even this slip," she whispered, slurring the words together. Her eyes were getting very vague and unfocused. "Maybe I'll let you take it off me . . . if you earn it . . ."

She dropped into my lap, plastered herself against me, and started in on one of her soul shattering kisses. She passed out cold in the middle of it.

For a time I just sat there holding her limp near-naked weight in my arms and not believing it. But it was true, too true. All the liquor she'd consumed had gone off like a delayed action bomb inside her and knocked her unconscious. And nothing was going to revive her, not for a long time.

I finally accepted it. Turning awkwardly, I managed

to stretch her out full-length on the leather couch. Then I stood up—wearily, regretfully, painfully—and wended my way out of the office, down through the thinning ranks of the party below, down in an elevator, and out through the downstairs lobby to the pavement outside.

It was night out. The darkness surprised me. I hadn't thought I'd been inside that long. I wondered what time it was. There was a watch on my wrist, but it would have been too much trouble at that point for me to focus on it. So I just stood there at the curb, swaying a little, waiting till a cab pulled to a halt in front of me. I climbed in the back, told the driver my address in what seemed to me a remarkably steady, clear voice, and fell asleep.

A hand on my shoulder, shaking me insistently, woke me up. The cab was stopped in front of my place. The shaking was being done by the driver. I climbed out of the cab slowly, dug a bill out of my pocket and gave it to him. Then I made my way into the building and up the stairs into my apartment.

I flicked on a light switch and trudged into my kitchenette. I'd already had too much to drink. But Penny Banks's conking out on me at the moment she did had given me a bad headache. It was in hopes that a nightcap would help that I took one of my open bottles of rye and poured a jigger glass full. But it was no use. The liquor already inside me rebelled at any more company. I barely managed to swallow half the jigger.

Setting the rest of the jigger down on the table, I wended my way to the bedroom, crawled out of my clothes, into my pajamas, and onto my lonely bed. . . .

Three minutes later I was sitting bolt upright on the bed, wide-awake, with the most violent stomach cramps I'd ever experienced clawing at my guts. Even then I knew it couldn't be just too much liquor. Liquor never hit me like that. I sat there hugging my arms hard against my middle and waiting for it to pass. It didn't pass. It got worse. Cold sweat began pouring over my face. And when a wave of dizziness suddenly swept through my brain, threatening to engulf me, I knew what had happened to me.

It scared the hell out of me. I scrambled off the bed, stumbled to the bathroom, and forced myself to throw up. It didn't help.

Doubled over with agony, my brain expanding and contracting like a bellows, hardly able to think, I staggered out of the bathroom and through the bedroom. I was halfway across the living room when a horrible extra twist of stomach pain dragged me down to my knees on the rug.

I stayed down there on my knees, panting and dry retching, fighting to keep myself from going all the way down, concentrating on the thought of the hospital three blocks from my place. I had to get to that hospital. I had to get there fast. My mind was disintegrating into meaningless fragments and my will power was going with it.

Desperately, I clung to the thought of that hospital. And finally I used it to drag myself up off my knees.

I staggered out of the apartment, down the stairs and out onto the dark pavement outside. There were buildings and people and cars and streets out there, whirling and wobbling around me in the blurring darkness punctured by the vague lights of the street lamps. I heard a man shout something at me. A woman screamed. Somebody laughed. I kept going. Battling to stay conscious and on my feet, I stumbled on through the night streets in my pajamas. I almost fell again going off a curb into a street, hearing the scream of car brakes near me. Somehow I got across the street. Somehow, I made it the three blocks to the hospital.

The wide stone steps leading up to the hospital entrance seemed insurmountable. But I mounted them, one clumsy, laborious step at a time, my legs heavy as lead and almost as nerveless.

The nurse at the reception desk looked up and gasped at the sight of me stumbling across the lobby toward her in my pajamas. When I got close, her head jerked back as she got a whiff of the liquor I'd consumed and her face got an angry, pinched look.

"What is the meaning of . . ."

I grabbed hold of her desk with both hands and hung on, feeling my legs going rubbery under me.

"Poisoned . . ." I moaned at her. "I've . . . been . . . poisoned!"

She must have thought I was drunk or crazy or both. She grabbed up her phone and began screaming into it for the police.

"Stomach pump!" I yelled at her over her screaming. "I'm poisoned! . . . Got that? . . . Poisoned!"

My legs went out from under me. I was still yelling that I'd been poisoned and she was still screaming for the police when I went down and out.

ELEVEN

I opened my eyes slowly and looked up at the white hospital ceiling. I felt empty, limp, burnt out and used up, like an old jalopy lying in a junk yard with its engine gutted out. But I also felt remarkably clear-headed.

I turned my head on the pillow. There was darkness outside the room window. It wasn't dawn yet. The lights were on in the room.

A doctor stood on the left side of my bed, watching me calmly. Lieutenant Sellers of Homicide stood by the other side of the bed, looking worried. They both looked equally tired. I opened my mouth to invite them to join me and get some sleep, but all that came out of me was a hoarse croaking sound.

"Don't try to talk yet," the doctor told me. "We've had to be pretty rough with you. Your throat muscles took a beating. Just take it easy. You'll be fine in a few hours. Your stomach has been pumped out. And we've administered drugs to counteract the effects of the arsenic poisoning. You're lucky you made it here as quickly as you did."

"Damn lucky," Sellers said. "Lucky you only drank half that jigger of rye. One or two full slugs, and you wouldn't've lived to reach the hospital."

I looked at Sellers and tried to ask him how he knew about the half-jigger. All that came out of me was another croak.

But he read the question in my face. "We've been to your place, naturally," he told me. "Found that jigger on your table half full. And the open rye bottle. There's enough arsenic in that bottle to kill ten men. The pint of milk in your refrigerator's laced with more of it. And there's plenty in the coffee in your open coffee can, too. Somebody wanted to make real sure you died, Jake, one way or another."

I nodded.

"Come on, boy," Sellers said. "Try to talk."

I tried. After a while I managed to croak out actual words. The words got clearer as I went along, but they didn't stop hurting the inside of my throat.

I told Sellers all I knew, all I'd done and what had happened to me.

He didn't look happy when I'd finished. I didn't blame him. What I'd told him didn't add up to any answers to what was going on. Somebody thought I was dangerous to him—or her. So dangerous that he or she had tried to murder me by poisoning. But the main questions remained: Who? And why? At the moment I wasn't up to even wondering about the answers.

"That had better be all for now," the doctor said.

"Okay." Sellers let out a disgusted sigh. He looked down at me and shook his head. "You're not much help, Jake. All you do is give me more problems."

"Sorry," I croaked.

But I wasn't sorry. I was glad—glad just to still be alive. It had been close. I shut my eyes and drifted back into a deep, peaceful, thankful sleep. . . .

It was late morning by the time I woke again. I tried to eat the lunch a nurse brought to my room on a tray, but it hurt the sore muscles of my throat and stomach too much. I ended by settling for the liquids—orange juice, milk and two cups of coffee. I felt pretty fair afterwards, but in no hurry to leave. The hospital seemed like a nice, sensible, safe place for me to stay for a while.

I spent the next few hours there, resting. Sometimes I got up and wandered around the room or stood looking out the window. Other times I sat up in bed leaning back against the pillows and staring at the wall, thinking over all that had happened since I first met Angela Hart and stepped off into a vast bubbling mess that seemed to have no bottom.

Maybe it was all the rest I was getting. Maybe it was that having so little food in my stomach made my brain clearer and more active than usual. Whatever it was, it seemed to me that the whole meaningless puzzle was beginning to take on definite outlines.

Four months ago Roland Miller had been murdered. He'd been keeping Angela Hart—a gal with too many bedmates—in style, but was beginning to tire of her and be interested in another model in his firm. Angela had had an alibi for the night of Miller's death: She spent that night with Ernest Lewis, in his apartment. Miller's wife, Nora, inherited all his assets, and her brother, Fred Usher, jumped from running a cheap clothing store to running Miller's prosperous business. But both Nora Miller and Fred Usher had alibis, too. They been visiting out-of-town relatives together.

So that should have been the end of it. Only it

wasn't. Because three nights ago Ernest Lewis had been tied, beaten, and finally murdered in his apartment.

On the same night somebody broke into the apartment of Nel Tarey, Lewis' secretary, to kill her. But she wasn't home that night. She was at the airport, seeing a friend off.

Also on that same night, a woman screamed in Lewis' apartment. It might have been Angela Hart, because by the time I first saw her in the Oran Club she already, knew that "They got Ernie." She came into the club looking for Steve Canby, one of her many old boyfriends. She was desperately in need of money to get out of town.

A thug tried to kill her after she left the club. I had her in my apartment when I got a phoney call that sent me up to the Bronx and left Angela alone in my place. The two thugs came to kill her, but she slipped out before they got to my apartment.

After that, my phone was bugged, probably in hopes of hearing something that would lead them to Angela Hart.

The next day an attempt was made to kill Nel Tarey with a stolen car.

That night Angela Hart had phoned me and asked me to come to her. This was overheard by the phone tapper. The two thugs got to her first, and killed her before I got there. They didn't live much longer than she did. But that still left whomever had hired them for the job.

And last night whoever it was had tried to murder me with poison, probably fearing that I was getting too close.

It seemed to me, as I reviewed all this over and over again in my hospital room, that I was close. Close to something that didn't fit right in the sequence of events, or something missing from it. I sat there trying to find the missing piece.

Finally, I found it. I sat up straighter and examined

it. It was an interesting question: How did whoever was after Angela Hart know I had her in my apartment three nights ago?

I'd come out of the Oran Club and caught the big thug trying to strangle her. I'd taken her away from him. I hadn't known him, and I was certain he hadn't known who I was, either. Not at the time. And when I'd driven away with Angela Hart to my apartment, I'd made damn sure no one tailed my car there.

So how come they'd known within an hour who I was and where I lived? They had known. There'd been that phone call decoying me out of the apartment. And shortly after I left, Angela had seen the two characters get out of a car and come up to my apartment, obviously in hopes of finding her there.

I mulled it over for a while. Until the nurse brought in my lunch on a tray. I tried a piece of toast and some poached egg and was relieved to find I could handle solid food again. It still hurt a little, but it went down. I forked some more egg and started it toward my mouth. And then I remembered.

The big killer I'd stopped in the act of strangling Angela. He'd come staggering out of that alley as I drove away with her. I remembered him gazing after my car . . .

I dropped the fork, grabbed up the bedside phone, and put through a call to a friend in the Traffic Bureau. I asked him to find out if anyone had checked on my license number three nights back.

He called back while I was finishing my hospital tray breakfast. The answer was yes.

Three nights before—shortly after I took Angela Hart out of that alley and drove off with her—a routine check had been put through to find out who owned the Chevy bearing my license plates.

The license enquiry had been put in by a detective on the Armed Robbery Detail, Harry Ross. My friend in the Traffic Bureau had already checked him for me. Harry Ross worked a night shift. He'd be off duty now.

I got Harry Ross' address and phone number from my friend, thanked him and hung up. I finished a second cup of coffee in a hurry, pushed the tray to the foot of my bed, and picked up the phone again.

I called Harry Ross' home number.

On the third ring, a man picked up the phone and said: "Yeah?"

"This Harry Ross?" I asked. "From Armed Robbery?"

"Yeah?" he said again, in a harsh voice.

I hung up the phone and got out of bed fast.

I felt light-headed and a bit shaky in the legs. But able to carry on, if carrying on didn't include anything hectic or physically punishing for the rest of that day.

TWELVE

It was a dreary six-storey building a block from the Hudson docks, in one of those tenement neighborhoods where you can hardly see the windows for all the wash hanging out to dry on the fire escapes. A bunch of kids were playing hockey with broomsticks and an empty beer can in the street, daring the cars that threaded through there to hit them. Their yells reverberated against the tenement walls on either side.

The building had once been elegant. Two stone lions stood guard on either side of the stone steps leading up to the open front door. The lions' faces had long ago been chipped away. Their dirty stone bodies were covered with names, hearts and various four-letter words in chalk, crayon and lipstick.

A teen-aged girl in tight green corduroy pedal pushers and a dirty white polo shirt sat on the bottom step listening to a soap opera via a portable radio held balanced on her knees. She was watching a tiny boy of

little more than a year toddle back and forth across the
pavement between her and a No Parking sign.

I climbed the stone steps past her and the defaced
lions, entered a narrow vestibule with cracked plaster
walls containing a wooden inside stairway, a public
pay phone and a coke-vending machine. Two six-year-
old boys were playing Zorro under the stairway, duel-
ing with radio aerials they'd torn off parked cars.
There were no mail boxes or any other indication of
who lived in the building.

I went back out to the top of the stone entrance
steps and called down to the girl sitting on the bottom
step: "Where'll I find Harry Ross?"

She went on listening to her soap opera and watching the baby as she answered me: "Third floor. Right
at the top of the steps."

As I thanked her, a bull-shouldered young man in
dungarees and sweatshirt came out of the saloon next
door, grinned down at the baby boy. He bent and
swept the baby up onto his shoulders and marched off
up the pavement with him. The girl got up off the step
and tagged after them, perching the portable radio on
her shoulder close to one ear.

I went back inside and climbed the inner stairs to
the third floor.

I knocked on the door at the top of the steps. In a
moment it was opened by a short, plump, gray-haired
woman in her sixties, wearing a flower-print dress that
made her look shapeless.

"Harry Ross live here?" I asked her.

She said, "Yes?" pleasantly enough.

"If he's in, I'd like to see him."

"My son just now went in to sleep. He needs his
sleep. He works nights, you know."

I nodded. "I know. But I have to talk to him. It's
important."

"Oh." She hesitated, looking me over, then backed

away, motioning me in. "Come in, then."

The room I entered was a combination kitchen, dining room and living room. Its furnishings were as old as the building, but the room looked very neat and clean.

The woman turned her head away and called back into the apartment: "Sonny! Someone to see you!"

Then she went to the stove across the room to stir something bubbling in a pot on one of the gas burners.

The man who shuffled through the doorway to my right was barefoot and wearing only a pair of pajama pants. He was in his thirties, a solid chunk of a man with a drill-sergeant's face and expression. He had short-cropped reddish hair, and there was more red hair on his thick-muscled shoulders and chest.

He looked at me blankly and growled, "Yeah?" His eyes were bloodshot, tired.

"Detective Harry Ross?"

"Yeah?"

I took out my wallet, opened it, and showed him my license photostat.

Something flickered in his eyes when he saw my name and what I was. But when he looked up again at my face, his face was still blank.

"So?"

I put my wallet away. "So I'd like to talk to you for a few minutes. In private."

He chewed the inside of his cheek while he eyed me a moment longer. Then he nodded. "In my room." He turned back into the doorway.

"Don't be talking too long, Sonny," his mother cautioned him from her stove. "You know how you are when you don't get your sleep."

"Don't worry so much, Ma." I could tell it was something he said to her pretty often. He went through the doorway down a narrow hall. I followed him.

We went into a tiny bedroom barely big enough hold a narrow bed, a chair, a closet and a bureau. The bed was rumpled. The bureau had been recently painted. A green shade had been pulled down over the single window to shut out the sun, but some daylight filtered in through cracks in it. Harry Ross shut the door, went around the bed and pulled up the shade. Then he turned and faced me, his face set hard, his eyes tough and cautious.

"Well? What'd you want to talk about?"

"You know my name," I told him. "So you know what I want to talk about."

"Don't play guessing games with me," he snapped. "I gotta get my sleep. I work nights."

"I know. Three nights ago you put a check through the Traffic Bureau on my automobile's license plate number."

He said, "So?"

"So I want to know why."

He turned away from me and took a pack of cigarettes off the top of his bureau. He took his time lighting a cigarette, then turned back to me slowly, blowing smoke out through his flaring nostrils. "Police matter," he said, shortly. "Nothing for you to worry about. Your nose is clean."

I shook my head at him. "Yours isn't. And your line's a phoney."

He squinted his eyes through the smoke curling up from his cigarette at me. He waited, saying nothing, showing nothing.

"Listen," I said. "I know how it is. A cop doesn't make much. There's no harm in making a little extra doing a favor for a friend now and then. As long as there's nothing illegal about the favor. I figure somebody you know contacted you that night, told you my license number, and asked you to find out who my car belonged to. Right?"

No response. I felt myself beginning to get sore. I looked at his muscles and reminded myself that I was in no condition to tangle with him. Even if it would have been the smart thing to do. Which it wouldn't have been.

"Listen," I tried again, "if that's the way it was, there's no harm in what you did. You just checked on a car license for somebody. All I want to know is who asked you for the check on my license? I promise I won't make any trouble for you out of it."

Ross took the cigarette out of his mouth and blew out a cloud of smoke. His face was rigid with stubbornness. "You got it all wrong, Barrow. That ain't the way it happened at all."

"So tell me how it did happen."

He shrugged like it didn't matter. "I was prowling that night and I saw this car come racing along doing around sixty through Manhattan. I tried to catch it, but I couldn't. I lost it. I got the license number on it though. Or thought I did. Anyway, I phoned in to Traffic and asked for a check on the number I got."

Ross cocked his head a little to one side and looked to see how I was taking it so far. I looked back at him stonily.

"Well," he said, "I found out the license number I had belonged to you, a private eye. And the description of your car didn't fit the car I chased. So I knew I must've gotten the number wrong. So I forgot about it. That's all there is to it."

"You're a liar," I told him softly. He stiffened. I saw the muscles of his shoulders swell, close to his thick neck. "There's a murder connected with this thing, Ross."

He blinked. "Murder?"

"Uh-huh. Somebody was trying to kill a girl named Angela Hart. She was at my place the night you checked on my license. Now she's dead. And there's been an attempt on my life. You can check this with Homicide."

His face had gone pale, his eyes unsure.

I pressed it. "You'd be smart to tell the truth, Ross."

But I'd already lost him. His face set stubbornly again. I'd scared him alright—into shutting up like a clam.

"Go to hell," he rasped, but keeping his voice down so his mother wouldn't hear it in the front room. "It happened the way I just told it. And you can't prove different."

"Don't be too sure I can't," I told him.

He took a short step closer to me, then stopped himself with an effort. "Time for you to go." His voice was shaky with the effort it cost him to keep it under control. "I gotta get my sleep now."

"Ross, come clean and I'll . . ."

"You gonna walk out," he whispered, "or do I drop you out the window?"

I shrugged. "I'll walk. Get yourself a good sleep. You'll need your strength. You're in bad trouble."

I opened the door and went out of his bedroom. In the front room, Ross' mother gave me a friendly smile, pleased that I hadn't cut into much of her son s sleeping time.

Outside the building, I strode down the pavement to the corner, crossed the street to the other side. The cab was there with its "Off Duty" sign showing. McCormac, a driver I used often, sat behind the wheel studying his racing form as usual. He turned his head to look at me as I climbed in the back seat.

"We wait, Mac," I told him.

"A tail?"

"Uh-huh."

McCormac went back to studying his racing form.

We didn't have to wait long. Harry Ross came out of his building and hurried down the stone steps. It hadn't taken him five minutes to get out of his pajama pants and into a suit.

"The one coming down those steps," I told McCormac, and held myself tense. Ready to scrunch down on the floor if Ross came our way.

But he didn't. He headed in the other direction, striding up the pavement away from us. McCormac started the motor, let out the brake, and eased away from the curb after Ross, keeping well behind him. Ross caught an uptown bus at Eighth Avenue. McCormac followed the bus.

Ross got off the bus at a stop a few blocks before 42nd Street, and walked east, moving fast. The cab ran into a traffic snarl. I gave McCormac a ten, got out and tailed Ross on foot.

He came to a halt in front of a corner saloon below Times Square. He stood there with his hands shoved in his pockets, staring in through the plate glass window. A tall, skinny man with a pale, bony face cut by a dapper, graying mustache came out of the saloon to Ross. He was nattily dressed in a white sports jacket with blue-gray tattersall checks, and gold slacks matched by the gold of his bow tie. His pale blue shirt matched the blue of the band around his soft grey crusher hat, which he wore with the narrow brim turned down all around.

I got into an office-building doorway directly across the street, where I could watch without being seen.

I was too far away to hear, but Ross seemed to be doing most of the talking. He looked furious. When at one point he dragged his hands out of his pockets, I saw that they were clenched into tight fists. The tall man dressed like a bad *Esquire* ad was being placating and looking worried.

After a few minutes of this, Ross made an especially angry point and raised his fist as though he were going to slug the taller, thinner man. But instead he turned abruptly on his heel and strode away.

The tall natty man stared after him, pulled out a

gold handkerchief and mopped his face. Then he got out a black cigarette case and a holder, also black. At that distance I couldn't tell if his hands were shaking. But it took a long time for him to fit a cigarette into the black holder, get the holder between his teeth, and light the end of the cigarette. Ross was out of sight by then. I was no longer interested in him. The tall man in the tattersall jacket and gold slacks turned and walked off. He carried himself erect, but his long legs dragged as though he were suddenly carrying too much weight for a muddy track. I drifted along behind him.

He led me to a smallish Times Square area hotel a few blocks away, its entrance sandwiched between a delicatessen and a bar. A sign in the window beside the revolving-door entrance advertised rooms for twenty-one dollars a week. I knew the hotel. Its tenants were mostly small-time show people, with a sprinkling of wrong-hunch horseplayers.

I gave him a few minutes, then followed him into the small, neat lobby. By then he'd vanished into one of the two elevators inside. I went over to the room clerk, described the tall man, and exchanged a couple dollars for some information.

The name of the man I'd been following was Henry Van Eyck. A big-time gambler, lately down on his luck. He shared a room and bath on the ninth floor with a woman whose first name was Lavinia.

"They *say*," the room clerk told me, "that she's his wife."

"Lavinia," I said. "Nice name. How about her?"

The room clerk nodded emphatically. "*Real* nice. A dish."

There was a door with a glass window in it, leading off the lobby directly into the bar next door. I used it. There were three girls and a guy on the barstools, talking show business troubles with the bartender, who wore horn-rimmed glasses. I found the phone booth in the rear, between two bathroom doors. The sign on one door said: Leading Ladies. The one on the other door was: Matinee Idols. Go to the john and goose your ego at the same time.

I got in the phone booth and put a call through to Van Eyck's room. I hung my handkerchief over the mouthpiece.

A woman's husky voice said through the earpiece: "Hi, who's this?"

Her voice stirred a memory stored in the back of my mind.

"This is Harry Ross," I said, talking hard and fast through my handkerchief into the mouthpiece. "Tell Van Eyck something new's come up. Gotta meet him right now. Same place."

I hung up the receiver before she could say anything to that.

Getting out of the booth, I went back to the door to the lobby. I stayed inside the bar, watching the lobby through the window in the door. In a couple minutes Henry Van Eyck got out of one of the elevators and hurried out through the lobby.

I pushed through the door and crossed the lobby to the elevator. "Ninth floor," I told the operator.

On the ninth floor, I went down a corridor with a worn carpet to the room number the clerk downstairs had given me. Lavinia opened the door at my knock.

The room clerk was right. She was a dish.

Tall and slinky. With hair like dark copper.

She had a perfectly chiseled face, knowing gray eyes, a patrician nose with a suggestion of passionate flair to the nostrils, and a wicked, to-hell-with-it red mouth. She was one of those lean girls that pack voltage like a high tension cable with all the juice turned on.

She leaned a shoulder against the side of the doorway and sipped at the drink she was holding.

"Well, hello," she murmured, her voice low and

foggy.

"Henry in?" I asked her.

"You just missed him."

"Too bad. I had something for him."

"Money, I hope."

"Better than money."

She gave a throaty laugh. "Nothing's better than money, boy friend. Believe me." She looked me over. "You could come in and wait. I think he'll be back soon."

I eyed her. She liked it. "A pleasure," I assured her, and stepped inside.

The room, dominated by a double bed, had a last-stand look to it. The carpet was worn thin, the original colors of the wallpaper had dulled with time, the two tall windows in one wall had a view of a brick wall across an airshaft.

Lavinia closed the door and finished her drink. "Have one while you wait?"

I shook my head.

"On the wagon?"

"Just for today," I told her. "I had something that didn't sit right last night."

"Well, I'm having another," she said. "A girl's got to do something to keep up her morale."

I watched her walk away from me across the room. She had the most exciting rear I'd ever seen, accented by the way the small of her back curved in. She took a bottle of bourbon off the bureau, poured some in her glass.

She turned to face me, raising her glass. "Well, here's looking at you."

I grinned at her. "More fun looking at you, Lavinia."

"You know my name."

I nodded. "Henry's told me about you."

"You an old friend of his or something?"

"Or something."

She sipped at her drink, eying me thoughtfully. "I hope whatever you want to see Henry about means some dough for him. It's getting so I don't know what money smells like anymore. Except in my dreams."

"That's a real shame," I said, making it very sincere and letting her see how interested I was in her. "Now I've met you, I can see you don't belong in a crummy joint like this."

She smiled at me, liking that. She returned some of my interest. "You a gambler?"

"Uh-huh."

"How's *your* luck?"

"Couldn't be better. I'm riding a winning streak that's lasted a month, so far."

Her interest in me immediately became more obvious. She drifted over to me.

"Trouble with winning streaks," she said, "is they let you down awful hard when they run out."

"Not me. I play the percentages all the way. That way, you always come out with something."

"You're a helluva lot smarter'n Henry, then."

I nodded, looking around. "This is quite a comedown for Henry."

"For me, too. He's all out of luck."

"He's lucky enough to have a doll like you. That's more luck than most guys have."

"Well, well . . ." she murmured. "I like you. You're good for my ego."

"How'd he ever manage to latch onto a doll like you? I can't figure you in a place like this. A girl like you should always go first class."

"Damn right! . . . But this isn't how it was when I first met him. That was a year ago, in Miami. I was doing a knife-throwing act with a guy in a nightclub there."

"I can see why you'd want out of that. Pretty scarey, having knives thrown at you all the time."

"Uh-uh. That was the twist in our act. *I* threw the knives. At *him*. I was real good at it, too."

I said, "Oh."

She grinned wolfishly. "We were doing alright. And then Henry came along. He was riding high luck back then. And he made the big play for me—jewels, a mink coat, champagne . . . the works. So I figured, what the hell, why work those lousy nightclub hours when there's a guy with all that cash to spend on you."

She watched the way I took that. I looked her up and down slowly, letting my pleasure show. "One thing I've got to say about Henry," I told her. "He always did have good taste in women."

She smiled, showing me her pretty white teeth, and the tip of her pink tongue between them. "I'm getting to like you more and more, boy friend."

She finished off her drink. "Sure you won't have one?"

I shook my head. She set her empty glass on the bureau and said, "Well, why're we standing around like this? Have a seat. Get comfortable."

I got comfortable on the room's only easy chair. "So you came north with Henry."

"Not right away. We went to Cuba first. Then to Las Vegas for a long time. That's where he ran out of luck, about two months ago. That's when we came here to New York."

"Maybe he's due to pull out of his bad luck," I suggested. "Now that he's got this trouble with Angela Hart out of the way."

All it bought me from Lavinia was a blankly puzzled look. "Angela Hart? Who's that?"

It was my turn to be puzzled. Up to then I'd been certain who Lavinia was.

"Angela's a girl Henry was having trouble with," I said. "Maybe he didn't tell you about her."

"I guess he didn't." Lavinia didn't look very interested.

"Well, maybe Henry'll pull out of his bad luck soon."

"If he doesn't pull out of it," Lavinia said flatly, "I'll pull out on him. I don't like living like this."

I let my eyes roam her again. "Can't blame you. A terrific girl like you deserves the best."

She ate it up. "That's what I like," she said, drifting closer. "The best." With a sinuous movement, she settled on the wide arm of my chair, her knowing gray eyes fastened on mine. "I wish I'd brought my throwing knives along. If I want to go back to work with another act, I'll have to buy new ones." She leaned closer, smiling down at me wickedly. "Want to be my partner in the act? I promise I'd never even nick you . . . if you behave."

"No, thanks. That wasn't exactly what I had in mind."

She laughed softly, deep in her throat. She reached out a forefinger and the point of her sharp nail traced my jawline, touching nerve ends that sent shivers to the small of my spine.

"I'm surprised you've stuck it with Henry this long," I told her. "Why have you?"

"No right guy came along with the right proposition," she murmured. Her fingernail traced through my eyebrow and down my cheek while her unblinking gray eyes gazed into mine. "If the right guy did come along. . . ."

"Henry'd be sore," I pointed out.

"You don't look like that'd worry you, boy friend. It sure don't worry me. Why, you know what that bum did to me? He even took back the jewels and the mink he gave me! Took them two days ago and hocked them for dough to bet on something."

"Maybe he'll win and you'll get everything back."

She made a face. "Not him. He'll lose that dough,

too. He hasn't won at anything in two months."

"What'd he bet your jewel and mink dough on?"

She shrugged. "Who knows? He never tells me about business."

She was leaning still closer over me, and it was making me damn uncomfortable. "I like you," she whispered. "You look like the successful type of man and I like successful types. A man should be success-ful . . . at all sorts of things . . ." She let me see the meaning of that in her eyes. "You look like you would be."

Her slinky body looked ready to coil itself around me. In another second that delectable rear of hers would have been in my lap.

Then Henry Van Eyck opened the door and walked in.

THIRTEEN

Van Eyck stopped short when he saw us together like that. Lavinia straightened slowly and stood up, not caring what he'd seen, or what he thought about it.

Van Eyck's pale face twitched. His dark eyes nar-rowed, moving from her to me as he slammed the door shut behind him.

"What's going on here?" he demanded in a nasty voice that sounded like he knew a lot of nasty ways to back it up. Close up, he looked less dapper and more like a brainy hood. "Who're you?"

I stood up and told him. "Jake Barrow."

It hit him. And I noticed that Lavinia, who hadn't responded at all to Angela Hart's name, responded plenty to mine. She looked almost as upset as Van Eyck.

"You dirty liar," she hissed at me, sounding shocked.

"Not about everything," I told her. But most of my attention was focused on Van Eyck.

His thinking was pretty quick. "*You're* the guy who called up here," he accused, "pretending to be Ross. To decoy me out of here."

"Sure," I told him. "That's a trick I learned from you."

His dark eyes got a guarded look. "I don't get your drift."

"Yes, you do. Ross checked my license for you. That's how you found out who I was and where I lived. Then you had me decoyed out of my place with a fake phone call, so your thugs could get to Angela Hart."

"I don't know any Angela Hart." It didn't quite come across the way he wanted it to.

"You knew her. She's dead. You made her that way. Like you did with Ernest Lewis."

"Why would I do that? I never met either one of them before in my life." He said that last part convincingly, which puzzled me.

I glanced quickly at Lavinia again, hoping to catch her expression off guard. But her expression was the frown of someone trying to figure out what was going on. Suddenly, I felt unsure. I tried to get a hook into Van Eyck again. "Don't play coy with me. I've got the whole picture. It started four months ago, with the murder of Roland Miller."

The hook didn't go in. I'd lost him. He even smiled a little as he shook his head at me. "You're on dream street, friend. Four months ago I was in Las Vegas, tending to my own business. And I got no connection with any of these people you mentioned."

"There's a connection," I said. "I'll dig till I find it. So if you're really clear on the killings you'd be smart to tell me what you know."

"Dig all you want," he told me flatly. "It's like I said. I got no connection. With you, either. So whyn't you blow?"

It wasn't a bad idea. I knew I wasn't going to chip anything out of him. And there were other ways, now, to find out more.

I walked past him to the room door, opened it.

There were two hoods standing in the corridor outside, facing me. One was short and scrawny. The other was of average height, but monstrously wide, about three-hundred pounds of powerful beef, bone and fat. The big one had the furrowed face of a pale ape. The short one had a small, thin face that retreated drastically above and below a long, sharp-pointed nose. They both wore loud checked sports jackets. They both carried guns in their hands, .45 automatics. Pointed at me.

"Back up," the short one said, calmly, in a voice that came mostly through his long, pointy nose.

I backed up. They followed me into the room. The big hood kicked the door shut behind them.

Henry Van Eyck was staring at them with his mouth open. His face suddenly looked like a bleached skull.

"Turn around, all three of you," the short hood said in a quiet, businesslike way. "Gotta frisk you first." He looked at Lavinia and grinned, licking his lips in anticipation.

"Benny!" Van Eyck blurted at the little man. "Please . . . wait . . . I . . ."

"Shut up, Henry," Benny told him calmly. "Time's come for your reminder. So take your medicine quiet, like a good boy."

"But you don't have to anymore!" Van Eyck's voice was choked with his terror. He looked at the big hood. "Just listen to me a second, Buff . . . Things've changed. I . . ."

Buff grabbed Van Eyck by the ear and gave it a little twist. "You heard Benny. Shut up."

Van Eyck grimaced with pain. Buff let go of his ear.

"All right," Benny snapped. "Now turn around and hands up high."

Van Eyck and Lavinia turned their backs to the hoods and lifted their arms above their heads. When I hesitated, both .45s instantly turned to aim at my stomach. Their depthless eyes told me they meant it. I turned around and put my hands in the air.

The little guy named Benny took my .38 with one expert smooth motion, leaving me no opportunity to do anything about it. Then he went to Van Eyck and removed a tiny .25 calibre revolver from his pocket. He saved Lavinia for last. Going behind her, he patted her slim hips.

"You can *see* I'm not carrying anything on me," Lavinia snapped.

Benny grinned. "I'd rather *feel*." His free hand roamed over her saucy buttocks. His fingers pinched.

Lavinia started to flinch away from him. Benny jabbed the .45 against her spine, stopping her. "Hold still for it, bitch," he ordered her, still grinning. For the first time, Lavinia began to look frightened.

The effort it cost me to stay where I was must have showed in my stance. The mammoth hood behind me, Buff, rasped, "You move, buddy, and I'll blow a hole in your back."

I didn't move.

Benny went on with his one-handed exploration of Lavinia. His hand went around her, fondling and squeezing each breast in turn, taking his time.

"You bastard!" Lavinia hissed through her teeth. But she held still for it, letting him do what he wanted with her.

His hand slid down over her stomach and lower. "Nice," he crooned, while she squirmed under his hand. "You'n me'll have to go on with this sometime, when I got more time." He smacked her rear in dismissal. "Okay, you'n this other guy back up against that wall over there."

He motioned with his gun. Lavinia and I got our backs against the wall, side by side. Benny stood facing us with his gun pointing our way, too far from me to be jumped before he could get a slug in me.

"Okay, Buff," Benny said without taking his eyes or gun off us. "Get it over with."

Buff put his gun away and started for Van Eyck.

"No . . ." Van Eyck begged, backing away till he was against the bed, his face contorted with horror. "Please! You don't have to, now. Just let me phone Gus! I'll be able to pay up now for sure. This Friday night. I swear it."

"We got our orders," Buff told him coldly. "You get a little hurry-up lesson. That's what I'm here for."

"Please!" Van Eyck pleaded. "Just let me call Gus and tell him I'll be able to pay him Friday. I . . ."

Buff shook his head. "Gus is a sucker for a sob story. It'd be a shame to let you hit Gus in his soft spot. Right, Benny?"

"Right," Benny agreed, without looking away from me. "Everybody knows Gus can't stand to watch people suffer. That's why he didn't come along."

The next split second Buff, moving with unexpected swiftness for his bulk, had hold of Van Eyck. Van Eyck didn't even struggle. He had a drugged look of accepting the inevitable. Buff bent him backward across the bed, pinned him down by sitting on his chest. With business-like unemotional directness, Buff grabbed Van Eyck's left wrist with one hand, his middle finger with the other hand. With one sharp movement of his hands, Buff bent Van Eyck's middle finger back till its bone snapped.

A thin mewing sound of agony seeped through Van Eyck's clenched, bared teeth. His heels drummed on the worn carpet. Buff shifted his hand to Van Eyck's little finger and calmly broke that, too.

Then he got off Van Eyck and said, "Okay, Benny,

that's it. Gus said two fingers, left hand."

Van Eyck slid down off the bed onto the floor on his knees, bent over slowly till his forehead touched the carpet, hugging his ruined hand to his middle.

Benny backed across the room, keeping his .45 aimed at me. He took my gun and Van Eyck's out of his pockets and dropped them on the bed. Then he glanced down at Van Eyck.

"I'll give Gus the word about Friday night being the payoff," he said quietly. "It better be the straight word. We have to come again, the next lesson is with crow-bar. We smash your hip bones with it." He motioned to Buff. "Let's blow."

When the door closed behind them, Lavinia relaxed with a long, angry sigh, went over to slump in a chair by the window and stare out of it furiously at the brick wall across the airshaft. She paid no attention to Van Eyck, who knelt on the floor by the bed, holding his swelling left hand and sobbing.

I got my .38 off the bed, slipped it back in the hol-ster and looked down at him. "What was that all about?"

He didn't answer.

"You tell me," I said, "and I might be able to help you."

He raised his head to look up at me. Tears streamed down his pale cheeks. "Private matter," he hissed through his teeth. "Mind . . . your own business."

"Who's Gus?"

"Get the hell out of here," he moaned. "Leave us alone."

I looked across the room. "Lavinia . . . want to tell me?"

She didn't speak or look at me. She was wrapped in a cocoon of fury, and still sore at me for conning her before.

I looked back to Van Eyck. "I ought to call the po-lice. They like to know about things like this."

Fear joined the agony in his face. "It was an accident." His voice was ragged with pain, but viciously determined. "I'll swear to that. Now . . . get out!"

I got out.

Down in the hotel lobby, I went through the door into the bar again, I got into the phone booth and put a call through to Van Eyck's room.

The phone rang five times before it was picked up at the other end.

"Who's this?" Lavinia's husky voice answered.

"Van Eyck there?" I asked and then concentrated on listening to her voice.

"He can't come to the phone right now," she said through the phone connection. "Do you want to give me a message for him?"

I hung up. I'd just wanted to be sure, and now I was. Lavinia might not have known Angela Hart, but hers was definitely the voice of the woman who'd phoned my apartment and decoyed me out to the Bronx three nights before.

It was almost dark when I left the hotel. I'd had it for that day. The poisoning and the stomach pump had taken their toll of me, and the emotion worked up in the session with Benny and Buff hadn't done me any good either. I felt shaky.

I found a cab and started to tell the driver to take me to my apartment. Then I changed my mind.

Somebody was out to kill me. The two thugs who'd murdered Angela Hart had waited to get me, too. That'd been two nights ago. And last night whoever had been behind them had tried to get me again, with poison.

There was sure to be another attempt. There were many ways to get at me. A gun waiting for me in my apartment or near it. Or a cute trick like dynamite in my car, hooked to the starter. A dozen other ways, and

I wasn't feeling up to coping with them at the moment. I decided it'd be a good idea for awhile for me to keep away from my apartment, my car, and my usual haunts.

I gave the cab driver the address of the hotel where I'd stashed Nel Tarey.

Evening was darkening into night when I got there. I took the elevator to her floor, went down the corridor to her door and knocked.

Nothing happened.

I waited. The door remained closed. There was no sound from inside her room. I tried the knob. It was locked.

I knocked again, louder. Called my name through the panel.

There was no answer from Nel Tarey.

FOURTEEN

MacLevy, the house dick, was behind the desk in his cubbyhole office, cleaning his fingernails with a toothpick.

The busy eyebrows over his sharp eyes raised up as I barged in through his door, and the rest of his beefy ex-cop's face came up with them. "Hi, Jake. Looking for your little girl friend?"

"Gimme the passkey. She doesn't answer her door."

"Simmer down, Jake. She ain't in."

It took a second to sink in. Then I realized I was holding my breath. I let it out slow. "Not in," I said, stupidly.

"She went out 'bout a half-hour ago. Hasn't come back yet."

"Moved out, you mean?"

"I wouldn't think so. No bags or anything. Probably just like last night."

"Last night?"

He nodded. "Went out last night about eight. Came back after midnight."

A terrible thought struck me. That would have given her time to get to my apartment with a load of arsenic . . .

"I told you to keep an eye on her," I snapped at MacLevy.

"I did. The rest of the time she's been in her room. No visitors, except you. No phone calls, in or out. Except trying to get your number. How's that?"

"She's not supposed to leave here."

MacLevy shrugged his heavy shoulders. "This ain't no jail. I got no authority to hold her here. And I can't tail her if she goes out. I'm supposed to stick around."

I sighed. "Okay. I want a look in her room. Right now."

MacLevy heaved himself out of his chair. I followed him out of the cubbyhole.

On Nel's floor, he opened her door with a passkey. We went in. He watched me case the bedroom and bathroom. There was no sign of anything wrong. Everything was as I'd last seen it, except that the beer cans were gone. She hadn't done a powder on me, anyway. Her suitcase and all her clothes and cosmetics were still there.

"Satisfied?" MacLevy demanded.

"I'll wait for her here," I told him. "Unless you've got objections."

"Not me. My morals ain't so hot, either." He went out and closed the door quietly behind him.

I paced the room for a while, alternating between fear for her safety, anger at her disobeying my orders, and acute suspicion of her motive for going out that night and the night before. I thought of a number of innocent possibilities, and some unpleasant ones.

After an hour passed without Nel returning, I began

to feel hungry. Leaving the door unlocked, I went out to a diner down the street from the hotel. I took my time with a hamburger steak, mashed potatoes and peas, drank some milk to sooth my aching stomach muscles.

Nel's room was still empty when I returned to it.

For a time I sat by the window in her room, gazing out at the night, trying to re-think Nel Tarey's part in all this. But I was too weary to work it out. And as more time passed without Nel's return, my fatigue increased.

Finally I took off my shoes, jacket, tie and shoulder harness, stretched out on her bed to wait for her.

Within seconds, I was sound asleep.

I woke with a feeling that I'd slept longer than I'd expected to. I was lying on my side. I opened my eyes and saw that the Venetian blinds were down and closed and the room was dark.

Then I heard breathing that wasn't mine and felt the weight of someone else in the bed with me. I turned my head. Nel Tarey curled up in the gloom beside me, wearing those black silk pajamas of hers.

I sat up and snapped on the bedside lamp.

She opened her eyes sleepily, and gazed up at me. Then she smiled slowly. "Hi," she mumbled. "Have a good sleep?"

"When'd you finally get in?"

"'Round midnight. It was a surprise finding you here."

"Where were you?"

"I went out to a double-feature movie."

"How about the night before?"

"Same thing."

"I told you to stay put here. I told you not to go out at all."

"I couldn't stand being cooped up here alone any longer, Jake. Where've you been? You promised to come back. I kept phoning you, but you didn't answer."

"I was out, working."

"Any luck?"

I started to tell her, then changed my mind. Her part in all this might be exactly what it seemed on the surface. Or it might be something else entirely.

"Not much," I said, watching her.

She looked disappointed. "That means I'm still stuck here."

"That's right. Only it seems you're not stuck here."

"I told you. I had to get out. It's too lonely, staying here all by myself all the time." She yawned prettily. And stretched. That was pretty, too. "I waited and waited for you, Jake . . ."

"Why didn't you wake me when you came in?" It was getting hard to hold onto my anger.

She smiled up at me lazily. "I thought you'd wake up when I climbed in bed with you. But you didn't. I guess you needed your sleep. Feel like your old self now?"

"You're not quite as simple as you seem at first," I said. "Are you?"

"You're angry at me. Don't be." She stretched again, holding it, letting me look at the way it raised and pushed out her lush breasts under the shiny black of her pajama top. "Don't be sore," she purred. "I always feel very loving when I first wake up. You should take advantage of it."

I was pretty soft with sleep myself. And a warm fuzziness was seeping through me as I gazed down at her. I tried to put a brake on my skidding emotions. Her arms reached up and wound around the back of my neck, and I knew it was a losing struggle.

"Listen . . ." I mumbled, weakly.

"No," she said flatly, and dragged me down to her. Her mouth went to work on mine with wanton abandon. Everything let go in me. My arms went around her automatically, under her pajama top. The skin of her back was deliciously smooth and warm under my hands. Our kiss became long and savage. My fingers moved to the buttons of her pajama top. . . .

She made an animal sound deep in her throat and pulled me back down to her. Her legs twisted against mine. I was all through talking or thinking for that night. My arms were full of smooth, soft, squirmy girl and she was moaning in my ear and there wasn't anything left in the world but our desire.

She was still asleep in bed, curled up like a contented cat, when I left her that morning. Outside, the sun was already dazzling. I had breakfast at the diner down the street, got a shave in a barber shop around the corner. By the time I got out of the barber chair, I'd sorted out the pieces of the puzzle that I knew and assessed the pieces that were still missing. In a clothing store off Amsterdam Avenue I bought a new shirt and put it on, leaving the shirt I'd worn yesterday to be mailed to my apartment.

Then I headed down to the lower East Side to find out more about Fred Usher.

The tiny store Usher had run till he fell heir to his murdered brother-in-law's business was in the second-hand clothing capital of the world. The few short, narrow, old streets are hemmed in by the Bowery, Chinatown and the Canal Street Arcade. It's crowded with a conglomeration of little stores, cellar shops and sidewalk pushcarts all peddling used clothing. The peddlers and storekeepers buy their merchandise from pawnbrokers, the Salvation Army, and rag pickers.

I spent the morning talking to the men who had been Fred Usher's competitors till four months ago. I gleaned a bit of information here, a bit there. Nowhere was I able to pry out a single word against Fred Usher.

Usher had been liked by everyone, and trusted as

an honest, fair-minded dealer by all. He'd bought his
store on Mott Street with the small amount of money
left over after his father's business ruin and suicide
many years before. And he'd managed to earn a small
but decent living from it, enough to support himself
and his sister, Nora.

When Nora married Roland Miller, everyone in the
district had expected Usher to move up into Miller's
business on Seventh Avenue. But he hadn't. He'd
stayed right there and continued to run his little store.
No one knew the reason, but there were guesses. The
most common guess was that it was a case of brothers-
in-law not liking each other. As it turned out, Fred
Usher didn't sell his store till Roland Miller died and
his sister asked him to run her dead husband's business
for her.

It was almost noon when I finished my prowl
through the district and dropped into a diner off Eliz-
abeth Street for a counter lunch.

I was washing down a sandwich of corned-beef on
pumpernickel with a cup of coffee when a short, stocky
man in a beautifully tailored blue summer business suit
came in. He had thick, wavy black hair going silver at
the temples, and large dark brown eyes that roamed
the diner till he spotted me. He came over and sat on
the stool next to me. His solid face was anxious.

The waiter behind the counter saw him and hurried
over with a smile of obvious pleasure, holding out his
hand across the counter. "Well, well! Mr. Usher! You
come back to do some slumming?"

Usher smiled faintly and shook the counterman's
hand. "Hello, Abe. Your coffee as bad as always?"

"Sure is," Abe told him happily.

"Then I'll have a cup."

"Sure. Black, no cream, no sugar. You see, I remember."

As Abe turned away to get the coffee, Usher twisted

his worried face around to study me. "Mr. Barrow?"

I nodded.

"I'm Fred Usher. You've been asking questions about me. Why?"

Abe brought him his coffee. "On the house, Mr. Usher."

Usher thanked him and waited till he went off to wait on somebody else.

"Well?" Usher demanded softly.

"How'd you find out about me?" I asked him.

"Several of the men you've talked to around here phoned me about it. They naturally wondered about it. So do I."

"I'm a private investigator, Mr. Usher. A couple people have been murdered. Angela Hart and Ernest Lewis. She was your brother-in-law's mistress at the time she was killed. Lewis was her alibi."

Usher looked startled for a moment. Then he nodded. "I know. I read about it." He turned his head and looked behind us. "There's an empty booth, Mr. Barrow."

We carried our coffee cups back to the booth, sat down across the table from each other.

"You think these two recent murders have something to do with my brother-in-law's killing?"

"I think it's possible."

"But why are you going around asking questions about *me?*"

"I told you," I said to him, "there's a strong possibility all three murders are somehow connected. And you had a dandy motive for one of them. Roland Miller's."

It didn't seem to anger him. He pursed his lips and studied me thoughtfully for a while.

Finally, he said quietly, "That is not a new accusation to me, Mr. Barrow. Others have said the same thing. No formal accusation, of course. Nothing legal.

But ever since my brother-in-law died I've been the victim of a sly insinuations that I had something to do with it. Or that my sister, Nora, did."

"If you didn't, you've nothing to worry about. Insinuations don't count."

"They hurt, nevertheless. Who are you working for, Mr. Barrow?"

"Nobody. Except myself. And cooperating with the police, of course. I got involved in Angela Hart's death by accident."

"Are you sure you are telling me the truth?" There was a sharp, lively intelligence behind his eyes.

"I'm sure. Why would I lie?"

"I thought of the possibility that you were working for one of my competitors. I'm sure some of them are responsible for all the insinuations about me and my sister."

"Your competitors around *here* seem to be very fond of you, Mr. Usher."

He sighed heavily. "Seventh Avenue is for bigger stakes. That seems to turn some businessmen into wolves." He fiddled with his cup. "Mr. Barrow, may I see proof you are what you say you are?"

I took out my wallet, opened it, handed it to him. He studied my license, gave back the wallet.

"I'd like nothing better than to have the murderer of my brother-in-law exposed," he said softly.

"That's fine. If you mean it."

"I mean it. As a matter of fact, I'm willing to pay you a bonus of . . . say two thousand dollars, if through your efforts, the murder of Roland Miller is finally cleared up, for good and always."

I finally had a client in this mess. I felt good. It always feels good to get paid for your work.

"The bonus sounds good," I told him, cautiously. "But suppose *you* turn out to be the one responsible for Miller's death?"

"I'm not."

"It could be your sister."

"She had nothing to do with Roland's murder."

"You sound very sure of that."

"I am."

"Good," I told him, "Because I'd like something in writing that says I get the bonus *no matter who* I find out had Miller bumped."

"There's a notary public a few blocks from here," Usher said. "I'll write out a statement to that effect."

"That can wait a few minutes. First you can give me some help. By answering questions. First of all, why're you so sure your sister wasn't responsible for Miller's murder?"

"Because I know Nora. She couldn't possibly have done such a thing."

I wasn't so sure. But I didn't push it. "How come you didn't sell your store and move up into your brother-in-law's firm until he died?"

Usher frowned. "I could have. Rollie offered me a good position with him, a week before his marriage to my sister. I didn't take his offer."

"Why?"

Usher shrugged a shoulder, looking uncomfortable as he tried to explain. "I guess I was too proud. I didn't want charity. And that's what he made his offer sound like. Also, I didn't want to work that close under Rollie. I never liked him."

"Why not?"

"I just didn't. Certain things I knew about him . . ."

"Like his reputation as a chaser?"

Usher nodded. "I don't like the kind of man who makes girls pay with their bodies for their jobs."

"How'd you feel about a man like that marrying your sister?"

"I didn't approve. But Nora wouldn't listen to me. She was tired of living in what she called poverty. It's not a nice thing to have to admit, but Nora married him for his wealth, knowing the kind of reputation he had about women. There . . . You see how frank I'm being with you on this."

I asked Usher more questions but didn't strike oil. He had no ideas on Roland Miller's murder—except that neither he nor his sister had been responsible.

"She'd have had no reason," Usher claimed.

"She could have been afraid Miller'd divorce her to marry Angela Hart."

Usher shook his head. "He'd never have done that. He was a rough, uncultured man who'd fought his way up out of the gutter. He liked having a wife with Nora's class. Besides, Nora would never have given him a divorce."

I nodded. "At the moment your sister seems very fond of a guy named Ben Massey."

Usher stiffened.

"Massey's a muscle-bound pretty-boy," I told him. "He was out at her place the other day."

"I know him," Usher said, distastefully.

"You don't like him?"

"Certainly not. I think he's a gigolo . . . if that's not too old-fashioned a term. He's only interested in milking Nora of her money. And I've heard rumors that he runs around with a pretty rough crowd here in town. Massey's not right for Nora."

"She acts like she thinks he is."

"I know," Usher said unhappily. "I've told her what I think of him. But she says she can't stand living all by herself out there. And she's dazzled by his looks. I'm afraid she might even end up by marrying him."

He looked up at me suddenly, a hopeful light in his eyes. "Maybe," he suggested, almost whispering, "Ben Massey had something to do with Rollie's death? Frankly, I'd be delighted if you turned up anything against him. Is it possible?"

"Did your sister and Massey know each other before Miller got killed?"

"Yes they did. You see, Nora is . . ." He hesitated, actually blushing, the color starting around his eyes and seeping down his cheeks. "Nora is quite vain about her figure. And Ben Massey owns a health club for women near Times Square. Whenever she was in town Nora used to go there for an hour's workout and a steam bath."

"And you think there was something between them before Miller died?"

Usher sighed and shook his head. "No. I don't really think so. Not till after Rollie died. Nora would never have been that foolish."

After some more talk that added nothing new to what I knew already, Usher took me to the notary public a few blocks away. He wrote and signed a statement promising me a two thousand dollar bonus if I was instrumental in solving Roland Miller's death—no matter who got hurt as a result.

Usher shook my hand briefly to seal the bargain, then hurried off. I put the notarized statement in an envelope, stamped it and addressed it to my lawyer, Max Wesley, to hold for me. I dropped it in a mailbox and headed uptown to the address Usher had given me—the address of Ben Massey's health club for women.

The reception room had dark mahogany paneling, pink plush carpeting, perfumed air, soft indirect lighting, and music drifting from a wall speaker.

There was nobody around so I crossed the room, pushed open a mahogany swinging door and glanced through. Inside was a small, neat-as-a-pin gym with the same perfumed air, pink carpeting and indirect lighting as the reception room. All the weight-lifting equipment was shiny with gilding, and the resting boards and the mechanical contrivances for rolling off fat had baby blue leather padding. Four women of various sizes and shapes were doing different exercises to change their various sizes and shapes. The green halters and shorts that they all wore were stained with dark perspiration blotches.

I heard the door in the reception room open. I let go of the swinging door and turned. A young woman of Amazonian proportions was standing behind the reception desk. She had short blonde hair and she was wearing the shorts and halter that seemed to be a uniform for the women of that club. Only her shorts and halter were dark red, and they had obviously been made special to fit her outsize figure.

She was six feet tall, with wide shoulders and hips. Very solid in front and rump. She had a flattish face with a hooked nose, and she looked strong enough to stop a truck just by leaning both hands against its radiator.

She looked at me and asked, "Can I help you?" in a voice as sweet and clear as a well-forged bell. Not a small voice, but nice to hear.

"I'm looking for Ben Massey," I told her.

Her face tightened, just a little. "He's not in at the moment," she said. "Perhaps *I* can help you, instead? My name's Dorian. I manage the club when Ben isn't here."

I shook my head. "My business is with him."

"Oh?" Her eyes studied me like probing dentist drills.

"Know where I can find Massey?" I asked her.

"No." She said it too quickly.

"Maybe he'll be back here soon?"

"I don't think so." The tip of her tongue wet her lips nervously. "I think he said something about going out of town for a while."

"I think I'll wait," I said. "Just in case you're wrong."

Something flickered in her eyes that told me I was right. "You don't have to do that," she said, anxiously. "You could leave your name and number. I'll give him a message to call you . . . *if* he comes in today."

"My business with Massey won't wait," I told her flatly. "So *I'll* wait."

She frowned at me, then shrugged, accepting it. "All right. But I'd rather you didn't wait here. It embarrasses our clients to have a man around."

"Massey's a man," I pointed out.

"Ben's different," she said. She didn't explain it. "There's a room inside where they wouldn't see you. Do you mind?"

"Not if you'll wait there with me," I told her. "There's some questions I'd like to ask you about your boss. I could make it worth your while, if you've got some answers for me."

She seemed to think it over. Then she nodded. "All right. Just a minute." She came around the desk and strode to the swinging door. She had strong, muscular legs to support her Amazon torso. She opened the swinging door a bit, looked in. Satisfied with what she saw, she let the door swing closed and turned to return to her desk.

As she passed me, she stumbled. She caught herself by grabbing my arm, leaned against me briefly.

"Pardon me," she apologized. "Very clumsy of me."

"That's all right," I told her. I was certain she'd felt the gun I was wearing. I was also certain that was the reason for her forced stumble against me.

"Wait here," she said. "I'll be right back."

I watched her walk through the reception room door, closing it behind her.

She was back in a minute, opening the door and holding it for me. "All right," she said. "The room's empty right now."

I went around the desk, past her through the door-way into a short corridor leading to a downward flight of stairs. Behind me, the Amazon closed the door. I felt a sudden prickle of apprehension, started to turn around to face her as she came up behind me.

Before I could get all the way around, she slugged her fist against the back of my neck exactly where it joined my skull.

Maybe she had something in her fist. Because the floor swung up at me and I dove down to meet it. But I was out before the floor and I made contact.

FIFTEEN

I could have used two heads to contain the ache crammed inside my one skull when I came to. There was a record player going, its volume turned up so loud that it, too, seemed to be jammed inside my skull. The number blasting out of the player sounded like it belonged in an album titled *Music To Go Limp By*. Which could have been my theme song at the moment.

I opened my eyes. For a while my vision was blurred, and the room revolved like a wobbly merry-go-round through the blur. Then the music quieted down a little, my headache shrank, my vision cleared. The record player seeped out of my skull and settled in a corner of the room, and the room slowed to a stop.

It was a small basement room, windowless and soundproof, its single door shut. The only furniture in the room, other than the record player, were several tall metal lockers and an iron cot with a thin mattress on it. I was on the mattress.

I was stretched out spread-eagle on my back. My wrists were tied to the top of the bed, and my ankles to opposite corners of the foot of the bed. I'd been stripped naked. My clothes lay scattered on the floor.

Dorian, the Amazon who'd knocked me out, sat on the edge of the mattress beside me, smoking a cigarette, still wearing her red halter and shorts.

When she saw my eyes focus on her, she took a deep drag at her cigarette, removed it from her lips, flicked off the ash, and bent sideways to touch its burning end against the bare sole of my left foot.

I yelled. My whole body arched up from the mattress, pulling at the ropes that held my wrists and ankles to the iron bed frame. The pain shot up inside my leg and exploded upward through my twisting body clear to the top of my skull.

She took the cigarette away from my foot, stuck it back between her lips.

"Okay," she said. "Now let's talk."

"About what?" I bleated. My naked body was bathed with cold perspiration. My left foot throbbed feverishly.

"Who are you?" she demanded.

"Jake Barrow," I rasped. "I'm a . . ."

"I know your name. And what you are. I looked in your wallet. What I want to know is, who sent you? Who's after Ben? And why?"

"Nobody sent me. I don't know anybody that's after . . ."

"You're lying!" she snapped. "I know Ben's been afraid of something for weeks. He's hardly been around here at all lately. He's been staying away. Hiding. I want to know what it's all about. I'm his sister. I've got a right to know."

"So get *him* to tell you," I growled. "And let me . . ."

"He won't tell me. But you will." She took a deep drag at her cigarette, removed it from her lips, flicked off the ash.

"Your feet aren't the only place I can burn," she warned me. "That was just a starter." She glanced down significantly at a very essential part of me.

"Wait!" I pleaded. "You're wrong about me. I just wanted to ask your brother a couple friendly questions about Nora Miller. That's all. I swear it."

She frowned at me. Then her frown tightened into a scowl. "I don't believe you. You're not the first one. There were two thugs here earlier this week looking for Ben. They threatened me. And then they . . . But I didn't tell them where Ben was. And now *you* come. I've got to know what Ben's afraid of!"

"I don't know!" I shouted at her. "I've already told you the truth!"

"Stop lying!" she hissed. "You mentioned Nora Miller, so that means you've already found out one of the places where he's been staying. You're after him. And you're going to tell me why!"

She took another drag at her cigarette. "I'm going to burn the truth out of you." She started the glowing tip down toward my cringing flesh.

The door of the room opened.

The sound of it stopped the cigarette inches from my skin. The Amazon jerked her head around to look.

Ben Massey came through the doorway into the room, looking bigger in his business suit than he had in swimming trunks. He took one step inside and stopped, stunned, looking at us. Then he took another fast step inside, quickly shutting the door behind him.

"What the hell . . . ?" he yelled at the Amazon.

She jumped to her feet, facing him, looking suddenly frightened. "I'm sorry, Ben. But I just *had* to know."

"Know what?"

"He came here after you, Ben. Like those other two I told you about. I had to know *why*. I . . ."

Ben Massey had been staring at me, shock on his face. Now he turned on his sister, his face going red with fury. "You goddam stupid jerk! When'll you learn to mind your own lousy business? Now you've done it!

We'll be lucky if we don't both go to prison for assault
and I don't know what else! How dumb can you get?"

Despite her size, his sister looked like a contrite little girl. She hung her head. Then her shoulders began
to tremble and she started crying.

"I'm *sorry*," she wailed. "I thought he was here to
hurt you. I was afraid for you . . . because you've been
so frightened of something . . ." Her sobs got wilder,
choking off her words.

Massey sighed and patted her shoulder in a resigned
way. "You can stop worrying about me," he told her.
"The heat's off. I just paid Gus every cent I owed him."

Her head came up, revealing her tear-stained face
and reddened eyes. "Was *that* what it was all about?"

Despite my position at the moment, it registered on
me. I watched Ben Massey nod at her.

"So you don't have to hide anymore?" she asked
him. "Everything's all right now?"

"Oh, *sure*," he drawled, sarcastically. "Everything's just dandy now. You've seen to that."

I tugged at the ropes binding me and growled, "If
it's not too much to ask . . ."

She turned quickly and looked down at me. It was
as though she were seeing me for the first time.

"I'm dreadfully sorry," she said, not looking at me.
"I thought you . . ."

"Will you shut up and get out of here!" Massey
yelled at her. "Go up and take care of the lousy customers. Maybe I can square this new mess you've got
us into."

She nodded and hurried past him, eager to do anything he said. When the door closed behind her,
Massey came over to the bed and stared down at me,
worried. He shook his head, rubbed his face with his
hands. "My God," he muttered. "Oh my God! Now
this. This's all I need."

"Will you for crissake get me loose!" I snapped at
him.

He nodded jerkily. "Sure, sure . . ." He bent and started to untie my wrists. "She . . . she do any damage?" he asked.

"Burned the bottom of my foot."

"Oh God! That dumb . . ." He got my wrist loose. "Listen, Barrow," he begged, "my sister . . . She's not very bright. Don't hold this against me. I . . ."

I sat up on the cot. "My ankles."

He bent quickly to untie my ankles. When he was finished, I looked at the small burn-blister on the sole of my foot.

Massey looked at it too. "It could have been worse," he suggested hopefully.

"It would've been," I told him. "In a couple more seconds."

I got off the cot and limped to my clothes, began picking them up and getting into them.

"She didn't really hurt you much," he pleaded. "Did she?"

"She scared hell out of me," I growled as I finished buttoning my shirt and tying my tie, got into the shoulder harness.

Massey stared at my holstered gun. "I couldn't be more sorry," he apologized sincerely. "She was just trying to protect me, you see." He was all sweet reasonableness now.

"Your sister," I told him, "ought to be locked up someplace."

He wiped a hand over his face. "Aw come off it, Barrow. Be a good guy, will you? She just made a mistake."

"Like the mistake *you* made, throwing those punches at me the other day?"

His unhappy face got still more unhappy. "I apologize for that," he mumbled. "You saw how it was. You're a smart guy . . . I didn't want to act tough with you out there. But I had to show off a little like that.

Nora expected it of me. You could see how it was, couldn't you?"

I put on my trousers, saying nothing.

"Can't we square this, Barrow? Somehow?"

I let him sweat while I put on my socks and shoes, got into my jacket.

Then I told him, "Maybe we can, Massey. Maybe. I'll forget it . . . in exchange for a little straight information from you."

"Like what?"

"Like what kind of trouble were you in?"

He was puzzled. "What do you care about my troubles?"

"I care," I told him.

He shrugged. "Okay . . . Well, I owed some dough I couldn't pay. I was trying to raise it, but I was scared I'd get worked over before I could get together the cash."

"Who's Gus?"

"Gus Banta. The guy I owed the dough to."

The name rang a bell for me. "Banta's a big underworld loan shark, right? With syndicate backing?"

Massey nodded. "That's him."

"I thought he operated mostly in Miami and Las Vegas?"

"Well, he's in New York now. Been here for a few months."

"He must've come in quiet. I haven't heard a whisper about him."

"This ain't Vegas or Miami," Massey said. "He's got to play it quieter here."

I nodded. "But just as rough. You must be nuts, borrowing from Gus Banta. With the tremendous interest he charges."

"Yeah. But he lends the money without any questions or security asked."

From what I'd heard of Banta, he didn't need security from his borrowers. He had a better guarantee of payment. Anyone who didn't pay up on time got a bad working-over from Banta's hoods as a warning. And if a couple warnings like that went by and the borrower still failed to pay, he'd be found in an alley or river some morning, unpleasantly dead.

"I was already in debt up to my ears for this place," Massey explained. "I tried to recoup by gambling and got in deeper. Finally I didn't have anyplace else to turn. And I didn't want to lose this club. So I made the mistake of borrowing what I needed to get out of hock from Banta. And when I couldn't make good on it, I really got scared."

"You had a right to be," I told him. "But now you're out from under?"

Massey nodded. "Paid Banta off just an hour ago." He allowed himself a small grin and added: "In a way, I've got *you* to thank for that. Nora gave me the dough I needed."

I frowned at him, not getting it. "How come I rate the thanks for what Nora Miller gave you?"

"I'd been trying to gouge the dough out of her before, but she kept playing it coy. Then like I told you, when you showed up I figured I had to put on the he-man act for her. Because I was afraid she'd stop liking me if I punked out. Only, the way it turned out, your knocking me cold was the best thing could've happened."

I sighed. "I still don't get it."

"Neither do I, quite. It brought out the mother instinct in Nora. After you left, she nursed me, cried over me. Really melted for me at last."

"And gave you the dough to get off Banta's death hook."

He nodded, grinning wider. "Crazy, ain't it? So I owe you, kind of."

"Pay me off in more information," I told him. "Do you know a guy named Henry Van Eyck?"

"Uh-huh. Gambler. Seen him around town a while."

"Know him any better than that?"

"Nope. Should I?"

I questioned him about Roland Miller's murder, and about Ernest Lewis and Angela Hart. Massey seemed quite open with me by then. But he swore he hadn't known Angela or Lewis and could tell me nothing that helped about any of the murders.

"Did Nora Miller know her husband was shacked up with Angela Hart?" I asked him.

Massey shrugged. "Nora always knew he played around with the girls in his company. I don't think she knew any of their names. And I'm quite sure she didn't give a damn."

Especially, according to Massey, after she met him. The way Massey told it, he and Nora Miller met at his health club, got chummy, and Nora was considering the possibility of getting a big alimony divorce by catching her husband in one of his love nests. But then her husband was found dead. And catching him with grounds for a big divorce settlement became unnecessary. Nora got the whole works without effort.

Miller's death had another result: It reversed the relationship between Nora Miller and Massey. Before it, she'd done the courting, and he'd played it cool, not wanting to end up with a broke divorcée on his hands. After Miller's death, Massey began urging her to marry him, and it was Nora Miller's turn to play it cool. Until my slugging him brought out in her whatever it is that causes one-hundred-and-twenty pounds of desirable woman to get protective about a hundred-and-ninety pound hunk of muscle.

Before leaving, I got Gus Banta's address from Massey.

"Please don't tell him you got it from me," he begged.

"All I've got for Banta are questions."

"Questions? For Gus *Banta?*"

"Uh-huh."

"If you know anything about Banta, you must be nuts." He shrugged. "Well, it's *your* funeral."

I limped out of the room and went to see Gus Banta.

SIXTEEN

It was a four-storey East Side parking garage. A perfect setup for an underworld loan shark. With all the cars going in and out all day and night, it would be impossible for anyone doing a stakeout on the place to know or prove which cars contained people going in to do business with Banta.

I went inside to the tiny glass-enclosed parking office on the ground floor. There was a large round hole for speaking through in one of the glass panels. I talked to the hefty young guy in coveralls inside, telling him I wanted to see Gus Banta.

It was the right place. The guy inside the glass looked me over carefully. "Got a name, buddy?"

"Just say Van Eyck sent me over. With the dough."

It didn't mean anything special to him. He picked up one of the two phones on his desk and dialed a number. After waiting a few seconds, he spoke into the phone, keeping his voice too low for me to make out the words.

His conversation was brief. He hung up the phone and turned back to me. "Go in the back and start up the ramps," he told me through the hole in the glass. "It's the top of the last ramp."

I walked back into the garage, squeezing my way between parked cars. It was dark in the rear of the place. A single, dirty, bare bulb shed a yellowish light on the ramp used for driving cars up to the upper stories of the garage. The air was thick with the sweetish smells of oil, grease and gasoline.

Hesitating between a Cadillac and a canvas-top truck, I eyed the lower ramp. If there was anyone at the top of it, he was hidden in the shapeless pool of darkness there. Taking the .38 from my shoulder holster, I transferred it to my jacket pocket.

I kept my hand on the gun in my pocket as I skirted a dust-thickened puddle of black oil and started climbing up the incline of the lower ramp. I was in no mood to take any more pushing around.

A wild temper is no asset in my business. I've got one, and I try hard to control it, usually with success. But when I get that certain feeling—the one growing inside me then—I know I'm just one step removed from losing control of it.

I couldn't think of anybody better to lose it with than Gus Banta and his playmates.

There was no one waiting for me on the dimly lit second floor. I walked slowly through the enclosed parking space half-filled with cars and trucks till I reached the next dark ramp. I sucked in a deep breath, let it out slow, and started quietly up that ramp. My hand was getting sweaty around the .38 in my pocket.

There was somebody waiting for me on the third floor, in the shadows near the top of the ramp.

It was Benny, the small hood with the big pointy nose. The one who'd done such a lingering frisk job on Lavinia in Van Eyck's hotel room. He eyed my approach, his right hand fiddling with his tie, where it could slide under his lapel for his gun in a hurry.

Then he recognized me. His hand didn't leave the vicinity of his hidden gun, but he grinned. "I remember you."

"I couldn't forget *you*," I told him. "Not after that show you put on."

Benny looked pleased, as though I'd complimented him. "Yeah. Buff's gonna be glad to hear his work got results this quick."

"Isn't Buff around?"

"He's out gettin' sandwiches and beer. How's Van Eyck feelin' today?"

"Like you'd expect. That's why he sent me with his payoff."

"Van Eyck's a smarty, payin' off this fast. What Buff did to him was his last warning, like."

"I guess he got the point," I said.

Benny grinned wider. "They usually do. Come on, Banta's waitin' for the dough." He nodded toward the next ramp. "You first."

"Sure," I told him . . . and whipped the gun out of my pocket.

Benny's right hand vanished under his lapel; his timing was phenomenal. But I had that split-second edge on him.

I slapped the barrel of my .38 across the side of his skull before he could get his own gun out. The feel of the impact and the thunking sound the barrel made against his temple gave me the first feeling of solid satisfaction I'd had in days. His eyeballs rolled up in their sockets. He collapsed like an empty bundle of clothes.

I caught him, eased him the rest of the way to the dirty cement floor. Getting his .45, I tossed it in through the open window of a parked Buick. I found a switchblade knife in one of his jacket pockets, brass knuckles in his pants' pocket and threw them into the Buick too.

I picked him up and carried him slung over my shoulder to the other ramp, began climbing. He didn't weigh enough to interfere with my keeping the .38 ready in my hand.

There was a small truck parked at the top of the last ramp. Behind it, artificial light shone through an open door in the cinder-block wall.

I went in fast, the gun held tight in my hand, my finger nervous against the trigger. The room inside had a single dust-coated window in one of its bare walls. Hardly any daylight filtered through that window. The room was lighted by a single bare bulb dangling from a wire in the ceiling. The room contained several chairs, a table with some whiskey bottles and glasses on it, a canvas folding cot serving as a couch against one wall, and a big old wooden desk.

There was only one man in the room. He sat behind the desk, toying with a letter opener with a heavy leather handle and a long, razor-sharp blade. His fat distorted the lines of his expensive sports jacket. He had a pale, bloated face and eyes that looked like they'd been chipped out of the center of an iceberg.

I dumped Benny on the floor, raised the gun in my hand a little, and said, "Hello, Gus."

Banta blinked, just once. After that the iceberg eyes in his bloated face stayed on me without expression. He put down the letter opener and placed his swollen hands on top of the desk. He'd become a little paler than before. But he looked about as frightened as a cobra studying a mouse he was deciding to make a meal of.

"What is this?" Banta whispered. "Who are you?"

I told him my name. It didn't seem to mean anything at all to him. He just looked a little puzzled.

"You lied to the boy downstairs," he said. "Van Eyck didn't send you. Whatever you want with me, this's the wrong way. Very wrong."

"You don't have to go out of your way to scare me. I know your reputation, Banta. Get up and come around the desk."

"You're making the biggest mistake of your life, Barrow," he whispered as he stood up. "From now on you're nothing but meat for the butchers."

He came around to my side of the desk. I frisked him. He wasn't wearing a gun. I thumbed on the safety of my .38 and stowed it back in my holster.

"How much does Van Eyck owe you?" I asked him.

He gazed at me impassively.

"I asked you a question," I snapped, feeling the pressure of anger swelling inside me.

"You poor dumb bastard," he whispered. "You got so little time left to you now. And you're wasting it asking me questions."

"You going to tell me now? Or after I beat it out of you?"

"You can't know much about me," Banta said. "I got friends that . . ."

"Your friends aren't here now. Just you and me."

"There was another brave guy like you that got rough with me," Banta said unemotionally. "About five years ago, that was. My friends heard about it. They didn't like it. This guy ran. They went after him. He hid. But they found him, finally."

"How much does Van Eyck owe you?" I asked him, and grabbed the front of his jacket.

"They worked that guy over with baseball bats," Banta went on as though I hadn't spoken or touched him. "Busted every single damn bone he had. But they didn't kill him. They were careful about that. He's been in the hospital ever since. Five years. He ain't dead, but he'd like to be. They got to watch him all the time."

The anger inside of me let go then. "Thanks for telling me, Gus. It puts me in just the right mood for this." I slapped him with a full swing of my arm, my palm smacking the side of his bloated face with a sound like a gun going off.

It spun him away from me. He whirled all the way around and fell back against the edge of the desk, his eyes and mouth wide open with pain and stunned surprise, the side of his face splotched by the blow. My backhand smashed against the other side of his face, knocking him across the top of his desk, drops of blood flying from his nostrils.

I grabbed his necktie with both hands and used it

to drag him off the desktop and yank him past my out-stretched leg. He tripped over my foot and sprawled face down toward the floor. His choked yell was cut short by the noose of the necktie jerking tight into his throat as he fell.

The ends of the tie almost ripped out of my hands as he hit the floor. I tightened my grip, fell on his back with both knees to pin him down. He jerked and flopped under me like a hooked fish. I hung onto the tie with my right hand, forced his head down with my left, and watched the necktie dig deeper into his fleshy neck as I pulled at it.

The sounds that managed to escape from him couldn't have been heard three feet away. His struggles under me became weaker. His tongue drooled out of his mouth. The flesh of his face and neck above the strangling noose turned purple.

I relaxed my hold on the necktie, loosened its knot at the side of his neck, enough for him to breathe again. Strangled gasps dragged in and out of his open mouth.

I let him fill his lungs a few times. Then I asked him, "Talk?"

It took time for him to get it out. But at last it came, choked words that sounded like they'd been dragged over a rough file, ". . . forty . . . thousands . . . dollars . . ."

I got off him. I stood up and lit a cigarette while I watched him. He clawed at his necktie till he got it loose, breaking off the collar button of his shirt in the process. After a while, he made it up onto his knees. Then to his feet. He stumbled to the nearest chair, dropped into it, sagging.

The ice in his eyes had melted. I'd taken something essential out of him: His belief that he was untouchable. Without it, he looked much smaller. Later, rage would come to replace it. But at the moment there was nothing in his face but a fearful humility.

I glanced down at Benny. He was still huddled on

the floor, out cold. I stepped to the doorway, looked out and listened. There was no sound of Buff returning yet.

I went back to Gus Banta. "All right. Van Eyck owes you forty thousand dollars?"

Banta nodded weakly, his frightened eyes watching me.

"How much did he borrow from you originally?"

"Thirty thousand," he gasped out.

"Ten thousand interest," I said. "Not bad. And he's paying up Friday night?"

"That's . . . what he told the boys."

"That's tomorrow night. He was dead broke, as far as I know, yesterday. Where's he getting the forty thousand from?"

"I don't know."

"Come again," I snapped.

"I don't know where he's getting it!"

I grabbed his necktie and started to tighten it again.

Banta's eyes glazed with horror. His hands clutched weakly at mine. "I don't!" he screamed. "For crissake! . . . I swear I don't know!"

I let go of the tie. Banta went limp with relief, his whole flaccid body shaking.

"I'd tell you if I knew," he rasped. "It ain't my business where a guy gets the dough he owes me. Just so long as he gets it."

Saying it stirred a memory of his power in him. Some of the ice began to creep back into his eyes. Just some of it.

"What happens if Van Eyck can't raise the dough by tomorrow night?"

His eyes slid away from mine. He licked his lips, not answering.

I said, "It'll be the end of the line for him. That it?"

Banta's eyes slid back to mine. He nodded, slowly.

"Okay," I told him. "That's all I wanted to know

from you. You could have saved yourself the agony by telling me in the first place. I'll be going, now."

"Enjoy yourself," he whispered. There was almost a threat in the words. He was getting his guts back.

I stepped over Benny's sleeping form and went out the doorway into the top floor of the garage. I started down the ramps, not taking my time.

As I reached the lowest ramp, I met Buff coming up it, his legs trudging slowly under the weight of his three hundred pounds of wide, solid beef. He was carrying a large bag of groceries in one arm. He stopped when he saw me coming down the ramp toward him, and looked puzzled.

"Hi," I said, grinning at him. "Sorry I couldn't stay to share the meal with you."

I went past him down the ramp, and out of the garage.

Gus Banta had sworn he had no idea where Van Eyck figured to raise forty thousand bucks by the following night. And I believed him. Which made me one up on him.

Because I was thinking of something else that was going to happen the following night.

Steve Canby's middleweight, Frankie Sims, was going to fight Rocky Gabe at Madison Square Garden.

SEVENTEEN

I used a drugstore phone booth to call Bob Sherman, a sports writer I knew.

"About the fight tomorrow night," I asked him over the phone. "Frankie Sims and Rocky Gabe. Who's going to win it?"

"You're not reading my column again," he said, "or you'd know. I thought you were my constant reader. Now I'm hurt."

"Your hunches," I told him, "have been known to

be wrong."

"Not this time. Frankie Sims to win is as sure a thing as you can get these days. There ain't a sports writer in town predicting it any other way."

"Rocky Gabe's no pushover," I said. "I've seen him fight. He packs dynamite in either fist. Got a lot of knockouts on his record."

"Sure, Gabe's a terrific slugger. But Sims is younger, faster, a better boxer, and he's got a longer reach. And he's no creampuff puncher himself. Maybe he can't hit quite as hard as Gabe, but his punches land where he wants them to more often. And he's got a darn good list of knockouts to his record, too."

"So you figure it's in the bag for Sims."

"Couldn't be more in the bag for him. The betting odds tell the story, Jake. Ten to one on Frankie Sims to win."

The top-floor dressing room of Knoble's Gym was reserved for the top-money fighters. It was a long, windowless room with swinging doors at either end—one leading in from the gym, the other leading to the showers, a resting room and a couple back offices.

I found Frankie Sims and his trainer, Doug McAfee, by themselves in the dressing room. Sims was face down on the rubbing table, his smooth tan-colored skin glistening with the liniment McAfee was using to massage his sleek muscles.

McAfee, his massive shoulders bulging out his polo shirt, worked over Sims with an expression of dedicated, tender concentration on his heavy face. He glanced up as I came in from the gym, nodded a hello.

I nodded back. "Canby around?"

"In with Alsberg." Alsberg was a fight matchmaker with an office in the building.

I looked at Frankie Sims, who lay utterly relaxed under McAfee's experienced hands, his eyes closed, a peaceful look on his face. "How're you feeling, Frankie?"

Sims opened his eyes sleepily, raising his handsome dark face and grinning at me. "Just fine. Never better."

"That's good," I said. "I'm thinking of laying a little bet on you."

McAfee laughed. "That'll be the safest bet you ever made, Barrow. My boy here's never been in better shape. You should've seen him out there sparring today."

"Don't use it all up sparring. The fight's tomorrow night, remember."

"Just light workouts today," McAfee said without interrupting the work of his hands loosening Sims's muscles. "To keep him in trim. Next we go to my place for a good steak, a lot of sleep. And tomorrow we just relax and save it up for the fight."

"Frankie staying with you?"

"Sure. The past two weeks. Gotta keep my eye on a valuable boy like this. Right, Frankie?"

Sims grinned over his shoulder at McAfee. "Your wife's almost as good a cook as my mother."

"Yeah, and she cooks what *I* say to feed you. Back home your mother'd be stuffing you all wrong. And your brothers and those girl friends of yours would be throwing you parties. You'd be a mess by fight-time."

"Where's home, Frankie?" I asked him.

"In Harlem. Place they call The Valley."

I nodded. "I know the neighborhood." I stood there watching McAfee working on Sims for a few more moments. Then I asked, casually, "By the way, either of you know a gambler named Van Eyck? First name's Henry."

Sims scowled. "Yeah," he said slowly. "We know him."

He glanced up sideways at McAfee. "Don't we, Doug?"

McAfee nodded. "Not likely to forget *that* one."

"Know him that well?" I asked.

"Just met the gentleman once," Sims said. "Once was enough. I almost lost my temper that time. Almost wrecked my future by hitting him."

"Canby did it for you," McAfee said, and grinned wolfishly at the memory.

"What happened?" I asked.

"This Van Eyck guy," Sims told me, "snuck in here and got me alone when I was dressing. Started talking about all the dough him and me could make together if I threw this fight with Rocky Gabe."

"When was this?"

"About three weeks ago. He said all I had to do was take a dive. He'd handle the bets for me, and nobody'd ever know. I got so sore . . . I was this close to slugging him when Doug and Canby walked in. So I told them what that crumb was asking me to do."

Sims grinned at the memory of it. "You should've seen Mr. Canby! Brother! I never seen anybody get so mad so quick. He hit that Van Eyck guy in the gut so hard I thought he'd never finish throwing up. And then Mr. Canby threw him out of here and told him he'd call the cops if he ever came back. Mr. Canby didn't simmer down for the rest've that day. Man!"

"Canby's got a pretty quick temper, you know," McAfee explained to me. "And this guy trying to get Frankie to throw the fight . . . With all the dough Canby's invested in Frankie. Well, you can't blame him for blowing his top."

"No, I can't," I said.

"I couldn't figure the nerve of that guy," Sims said, "having the guts to come in here and proposition me like that. But Mr. Canby said he'd heard Van Eyck was a gambler who'd gotten himself into bad trouble, owing dough to a guy that'd bump him off if he didn't pay. So Mr. Canby guessed he was desperate."

I nodded slowly, puzzling it out as I watched them

go on with the rubdown. After a few minutes I motioned goodbye to them and went through the other swinging door to the back.

The door to the matchmaker's office had black lettering on its frosted glass that read: G. Alsberg—Promotions. I opened the door and went in.

It was a small room, with nothing in it but an old table, several kitchen chairs, and walls covered with photographs of boxers. Steve Canby and Alsberg sat at the table, playing gin rummy. Alsberg was a small man with a completely bald head and a very wrinkled face. He looked and dressed like a charity case. The rumor was that he was worth half-a-million dollars.

"Some business conference," I said, interrupting their concentration on the cards.

They both looked up and grinned at me. Canby's face didn't lose its perpetually anxious look even when he smiled.

"How're'ya, Jake," he said. "What're you doing around here?"

"Having a look at your fighter, Steve. He's pretty confident about tomorrow night."

"He knows he's gonna win," Canby said.

"So does everybody else," Alsberg complained. "That's what I'm worried about. Not much money in a sure-thing fight. Who wants to pay good money to attend a fight they figure's that one-sided?"

"You'll have a good attendance," Canby said. "Don't worry. Everybody likes to watch Frankie in action. And Rocky Gabe being such a slugger, he's got lots of fans, too. There'll be a good gate, don't worry."

"I always worry when I set up a match. My reputation's at stake each time. One nothing-fight, and I'm marked lousy for months."

"I'd like to talk to you, Steve," I said. "It's sort of private."

Alsberg put his cards down on the table and stood up. "Gotta go to the can for about fifteen minutes.

Don't peek at my hand, you crook."

He shuffled out, closing the door behind him.

"What's up?" Canby asked me.

"Sims and McAfee were telling me about what happened with Van Eyck."

Anger twisted his face briefly. Then he forced a rueful grin. "Christ! I still get mad, remembering it. Ain't that crazy? I've had plenty of time to calm down about it. But, boy, I was really sore at the time."

"So they told me."

He nodded. "Yeah. I really lost my head. Him having the nerve to proposition one of my boys like that. But I guess in a way, it was kind of funny."

"Funny?"

"Him being nuts enough to think Frankie'd even consider it. Hell, even just financially, there'd be no more percentage in it for Frankie than there'd be for me. No matter how much dough bets'd bring in from throwing the fight, it wouldn't match what'd be lost in the long run. I got a champ in Frankie, and he knows it. Both of us're gonna make a fortune—a real fortune—off his fights in the next few years. But all that'd be lost if he threw this fight. He wouldn't get the crack at the championship if he lost to Gabe."

He suddenly frowned at me. "How come you're interested in Van Eyck?"

"I think he's connected with Angela Hart."

"How?"

"I'm not quite sure, yet. All I can be sure of is that he had something to do with her death. And I can't even prove that. Yet."

Canby's eyes clouded. He looked down at his clenched fists on the table, chewed his lip for a moment. "I read about Angela getting it," he muttered finally. "In the papers. A rotten shame . . . but I can't say I was surprised."

I tensed. "You know a reason somebody'd have to

murder her?"

He looked up at me, startled. "No . . . Nobody special. Just the general thing I told you about before. I'd bet dough it was one of the guys she had on her string. She always had too many of them, like I told you before. Remember? I told you whatever trouble she was in had to be man-trouble."

I nodded. "I remember. You told me."

"She was a nympho, I guess . . . Went for anything in pants."

"How about Van Eyck? Was he one of her men?"

Canby shrugged. "Search me. If he was, I never heard about it. But then she had lots of guys I didn't know about. No guy could resist her when she went to work on him. Hardly any guy," he added, thinking about it. "Frankie did."

I stared at him. "Frankie Sims?"

He nodded unhappily. "Yeah. That was back when she was supposed to be going with me. She made a play for Frankie, behind my back. I told you I decided she wasn't good for me, so I dropped her. Well, that was what made up my mind for me. I had it bad for her, but I couldn't take that kind of crap." He shook his head angrily, remembering. "She didn't get anywhere with Frankie, though. I could've told her she wouldn't. Frankie takes his training seriously. And he's kind of a prude, too. But she sure tried."

"How well do you know Van Eyck?" I asked him.

"Just what I hear around."

"He's in pretty bad trouble," I said.

"So I hear. He deserves it."

We talked a little more, but Canby didn't have anything more to tell me. When Alsberg returned, I left.

Doug McAfee was alone in the dressing room now when I returned.

"Where's Frankie?" I asked him.

"Showers. Time for him to get dressed and go home with me."

I grinned at him. "You'd have made a good mother, McAfee."

He nodded, seriously. "Or father. I never had a son. I'd be a good father."

I perched on the edge of the rubbing table, looking at McAfee, toying with a hunch based on what I'd learned so far about Angela Hart.

I played the hunch: "Canby tells me you and Angela Hart used to have a thing for each other."

The dart struck the target. He looked up sharply at me. "What makes that any of your business?"

"She's dead."

"I know. I read the papers too."

"I'm trying to find out who killed her," I told him.

"You think maybe *I* did?"

"I'm interested in anybody who knew her. Anybody who knew anything *about* her. You knew her pretty well."

He shook his head. "Wrong. Not well. I knew her. But it didn't amount to much."

It amounted to enough to bring shame to his face.

"Maybe I didn't hear it right before," I said. "Suppose you tell me how it really was."

"She went for any man around." McAfee shoved his hands in his pockets—maybe to keep himself from using his fists on me. He stood with his feet set apart, staring at me with tough, unhappy eyes, his massive shoulders slumping.

"I knew I shouldn't touch her," he muttered, softly. "She was Canby's girl. Supposed to be. Anyway, he was nuts about her. But she . . . she was kind of too much for me. Made a pass at me one night. Right here in the gym, after everybody else'd gone. And backed the pass up, if you know what I mean."

"I think I do," I told him, remembering the way she'd been with me, the first night I met her.

"I just couldn't stand her off like I knew I should,"

McAfee confessed, shamefaced. "She was pretty terrific. And I guess she was all worked up from trying to make Frankie and not being able to. She was like that. Sexiest girl I ever met."

"So that was the start of it between you and her?" I suggested, feeling my way.

McAfee looked puzzled. "The start? There wasn't anything after. That was it, right here that night. And it didn't get very far, at that."

"How come?"

"Canby came back in here looking for her."

"And caught her with you?"

McAfee nodded. "He went nuts for a couple minutes. That temper of his really let go. Started swinging at me like he wanted to kill me."

"You look to me like you wouldn't have any trouble handling Canby," I said.

"Oh, sure. I could've knocked him kicking real easy. But I didn't. I felt too guilty about messing around with his girl. So I just tangled him up and held him till he calmed down. He was sorry about it, after he did simmer down. He knew damn well I wasn't to blame. It was her fault. After that he stopped seeing her. Which was a damn good thing. She had him upset all the time."

"I thought he stopped seeing her because she made a play for Frankie Sims?"

"That, too. It was hard for him to give her up, even when he wanted to, you see. We had a couple of drinks together after that tussle we had and he told me about it. He couldn't get her out of his system. He finally did, but it was hard-going."

"*Did* he get her out of his system?"

"Oh, sure," McAfee said, emphatically. "Finally. He started playing around with other broads. That's what did it for him. Angela dropped around here once. Afterwards. To borrow dough from Canby, or something. You could see, just looking at them, that he didn't give a damn about her anymore. He loaned her the money, but just to get rid of her."

I left McAfee and went out of the gym. Outside, the dark of evening was settling into the canyons of Manhattan.

It had been a long, involved day. I was getting tired and hungry. But I was too close to it to stop now.

EIGHTEEN

I dropped into a tavern a few blocks from the gym. Sitting in a dimly lighted booth, making a meal of a steak sandwich and a bottle of beer, I examined the pieces of my human jigsaw puzzle.

The pieces had names—and were related to each other, in various ways:

Angela Hart had had a lover named Ernest Lewis, a photographer with a secretary named Nel Tarey.

Angela Hart had had another lover, Steve Canby, who in turn had a fighter named Frankie Sims and a trainer named Doug McAfee.

Angela Hart had had still another lover named Roland Miller, a dress manufacturer with a wife named Nora, a brother-in-law named Fred Usher, plus a lot of other girl friends in his firm. Not to mention a handsome fellow named Ben Massey, who was playing around with Miller's wife and had a batty Amazon for a sister.

Angela Hart had had two killers after her. Their trail led to a cop named Harry Ross, who led in turn to a broke gambler named Henry Van Eyck. Van Eyck had an ex-knife-thrower girl friend named Lavinia, who was sore at him for being broke. Also, an underworld loan-shark named Gus Banta was going to kill him unless he coughed up forty thousand dollars.

I shifted around these pieces in my mind as I ate,

trying to fit each piece into its proper place in the puzzle. By the time I finished my steak sandwich and was working on the last of my beer, I knew there were a couple pieces still missing.

I concentrated on one of the pieces that I did have: Van Eyck.

Van Eyck had to come up with forty thousand dollars for Gus Banta or he was a dead man.

He'd taken back Lavinia's jewels and fur, hocked them for money to bet on something.

And he'd promised to pay Gus Banta by Friday night, tomorrow night—knowing he'd be killed if he missed that deadline.

I knew of one thing he could be betting on Friday night—the Frankie Sims-Rocky Gabe fight.

But if I was right, how could Van Eyck be expecting to pay off Banta with his winnings? Frankie Sims was supposed to be a cinch to win. The betting odds were ten-to-one that he would. Van Eyck would have to bet four hundred thousand dollars on Sims, to win the forty thousand he needed at those odds. He certainly didn't have four hundred thousand bucks, or he'd have paid off his debt to Banta long ago. Besides which, no matter how many jewels he'd given to Lavinia in his plush days, they wouldn't hock worth almost half-a-million.

They wouldn't even hock worth forty thousand, or he'd have paid off Banta with it.

Which left the other possibility: With the odds ten-to-one that Frankie Sims would win, Van Eyck would only have to bet four thousand dollars *against* Sims to make the forty thousand he needed—*if Frankie Sims lost*. And it was quite probable that Lavinia's jewels and mink would hock worth four thousand.

The only trouble with that line of reasoning was that everyone who should know was certain that Frankie Sims would not lose. That he was a cinch to beat Rocky Gabe.

Which brought me back to where I'd started. And left the strong possibility that my thinking was way off in the wrong side of the field. I could be just trying to force together two things which didn't really belong together. The fact that Van Eyck was expecting to have enough to pay his debt Friday night, and that the fight was also Friday night, could be just a coincidence. And probably was.

On the other hand. . . .

I went to the phone booth in the rear of the tavern and put through another call to my sports writer friend, Bob Sherman.

"What now?" he asked through the phone.

"The Sims-Gabe fight tomorrow night, again," I told him. "Is there any possibility that it's a setup? That Frankie Sims might take a dive?"

I asked it, though I didn't really believe in it.

Neither did Sherman. "No possibility at all, Jake. First of all, all the smart money is on Sims to win. And that includes the bets of the fight-racket mobsters, who'd be in the know if there was a setup going. Second of all, neither Sims nor his manager, Steve Canby, are that kind of guys. They've both got clean records. Finally, it wouldn't pay either of them. Not in the long run. Sims wins tomorrow night, and he goes on to take the championship. Both he and Canby stand to make more out of that than either of them could make out of a dive tomorrow night."

I nodded to myself in the phone booth. Steve Canby had said almost exactly the same thing.

"Thanks for the information," I told Sherman. "Can you get me a ticket to the fight tomorrow night? Pretty close to ringside?"

"I think so. But it'll cost you."

"That's okay. I'll get the ticket from you sometime tomorrow. And thanks again."

I hung up and sat there in the booth for a few moments, absorbing it. According to Sherman, there was no chance that the Sims-Gabe fight was a setup. According to everyone else, too.

But I knew of one man who'd know the truth better than any of them.

I left the tavern and went up to Harlem to search for him

His name was Ace. I'd once gotten his sister out of a jam.

Ace lived and worked in "The Valley"—a Harlem neighborhood where Frankie Sims's family also happened to live. He was a middle-aged bachelor who in his twenties had gotten a degree from Columbia University. Unfortunately for him, he got his degree in architecture, a pursuit in which a Negro had as much chance to get ahead as a fifty-year-old prostitute has of getting invited to a debutante's ball.

So Ace was a bookie, among other things. The other things included running a Harlem institution known as "gambling parties." Ace would rent someone's apartment, for one night. The people in it moved out to spend the night with various relatives and friends—and Ace moved in with a big poker or craps game. By renting a different apartment each time, the gamblers ran less risk of the cops finding them and breaking up the game.

Ace had something to do with any kind of gambling that went on in The Valley. And the betting that he didn't handle, he knew about. So I went to see Ace.

Ace's apartment was in a neat, well-tended building in a block where the other buildings weren't so neat and well-tended. Ace wasn't in, and his landlady had no idea where he was.

I went to a candy store a few blocks away where Ace could often be found, inside or hanging around out on the corner, where hunch players could find him when they wanted to make bets. He wasn't there, either. Which meant he was probably throwing one of his "parties" somewhere. I asked around for a while, trying to find out where his party was that night. But I didn't really expect to find out. And I didn't.

I finally went back to his building and persuaded the landlady to let me into his apartment to wait for him. The persuasion consisted mostly of a three-dollar bribe.

I wandered around his well-furnished apartment for a while, used up some of his liquor, made myself a sandwich from his refrigerator, listened to some albums on his hi-fi system he'd built himself into one of the closets. It was one o'clock in the morning when I stretched out on his bed and went to sleep.

The first light of dawn was showing at the open bedroom windows when he woke me coming in.

He didn't look surprised to see me. Ace had long ago learned to take life as it came to him, minute by minute. And he didn't expect it to bring him presents. He was a tall, solid man with an expression of unvarying dignity. I'd first met him during a time that was causing him a lot of emotional pain, but he'd never lost that calm expression of his once, even in those circumstances. I was one of the few who knew about his ulcers.

"I heard that you were looking for me, Jake. But I couldn't leave the game. I was too much ahead. Have a good sleep?"

I sat up and swung my shoes down to the floor, rubbed my face with hands and nodded. "Feels like I had enough. You must be bushed."

"Very. I've got coffee perking."

I went into the bathroom and used cold water on my face and neck to get rid of my grogginess. Then I shaved quickly, went out to his kitchen, sat down to coffee and fresh buttered rolls with him, and asked him what I'd come to ask.

"How're they betting around Sims-Rocky Gabe fight tonight?"

"Like prosperity is back."

"On Frankie to win."

"Of course," Ace said. He didn't ask me why the questions.

"That's how everybody feels downtown, too," I said. "Odds are ten-to-one."

"Around here you have to give a man fifteen-to-one to get him to bet against Frankie Sims."

"How're you betting?"

"I'm not," Ace told me. "It would be throwing money away to bet against Frankie. And the other way the odds are too steep, and upsets have been known to happen."

"Yes. They have. How about Frankie Sims's family? Any of them putting out any money on the fight?"

"All of them. His mother and his four brothers. Also his uncles and his cousins whom he reckons by the dozens and his aunts." He hadn't asked me, but he knew what I wanted to know: "On Frankie to win."

"You know this for a fact? Not just rumor?"

"It is a fact."

So there it was. Frankie Sims wasn't going to throw the fight. I hadn't actually thought he would. But I'd had to be sure of what I did think.

As I walked out into the empty dawn streets of Harlem and strolled toward the subway, I was sure.

The emptiness of the streets and the coolness of the early morning air made my head feel very clear. I went over the pieces of my jigsaw puzzle again, slowly, dropping each one into place.

Angela Hart had had three lovers that I knew about: Ernest Lewis, Steve Canby and Roland Miller. Now Lewis and Miller were dead. That left Steve Canby.

The two killers who had been after Angela Hart

had been hired for the job by Van Eyck. The fact that Harry Ross went straight to Van Eyck after I threw a scare into him could have been a coincidence. He might have gone to see Van Eyck about something else entirely. But the fact that it was Van Eyck's girl friend, Lavinia, who'd called me on the phone and decoyed me out of my apartment to leave Angela Hart there alone—that was no coincidence.

So there they were: Steve Canby and Van Eyck—Van Eyck with a big chunk of cash to raise that night, and Canby with a fighter going into the ring with the odds riding on him, also that night.

And by then I thought I knew what connected the two men—the reason for what had been happening, the different motives that linked the diverse parts together.

I had all the pieces of my jigsaw puzzle in place now. All except one. I was counting on the fight at Madison Square Garden to drop that final piece into place for me. . . .

I was wearing my gun when I went to the Garden that night.

NINETEEN

Alsberg, the matchmaker, had been right about the gate. The Garden hadn't packed in too much of a crowd that night. Many fans had stayed away, figuring that with the odds riding so heavy in Frankie Sims's favor, it wasn't going to be much of a contest. Much of the crowd that was there had been attracted by Rocky Gabe's reputation as a slugger and a guy who took a lot of punishment without going down. The bloodthirsty crowd. They'd come to watch Gabe stand up to fifteen rounds of being cut to ribbons—with the added spice that Gabe had the punch to land a hay-maker and pull an upset.

I got there as the last prelim before the main event was finishing—two unpromising heavyweights who climbed out of the ring after their last round with the weary slowness of old men who were way past their bedtime. Bob Sherman had gotten me a good seat, on the aisle seven rows back from the ring. As I sat down I saw Sherman sitting further down the same aisle, at ringside. Which might turn out to be a help. . . .

Frankie Sims got a pretty good cheer from the crowd as he came down the aisle and climbed into the ring, followed by Doug McAfee and Steve Canby, who were acting as his seconds for this fight. Sims looked good, grinning confidently and walking with a quick, springy step.

Rocky Gabe and his seconds came in next. Gabe was a good four inches shorter than Sims, and about ten years older. But his solid, heavy-muscled build re-vealed more obvious power than Sims showed. He was balding around his low forehead, and his face, marked by the scars and distortions of eleven years of battling, was pale. He got a little handclapping and a lot of boos as he climbed into the ring. But his expression of grim patience didn't alter as he looked across the ring at Sims.

I sat on the edge of my chair, anxious for the fight to begin.

It started the way it had been predicted. Three sec-onds after the starting bell for the first round, Frankie Sims connected with a long left jab that brought a trickle of blood from Rocky Gabe's battered nose and sent his head snapping back. Sims stepped in fast and followed it with a sharp right cross to the side of the head and a left hook to the mid-section which forced Gabe to fall back a few steps. When Sims followed him, Gabe tried to tag him with a full-swinging hay-maker right. Sims side-stepped the punch and slashed a one-two to Gabe's mouth. Gabe took it and slammed a short hard left into Sims's heart that knocked him away. But when Gabe charged in and tried to follow it up, Sims danced away from him effortlessly.

It went that way for the rest of the first round. Sims dancing all around Gabe and slashing him with lefts and rights that weren't enough to put the Gabe down, but carried plenty of sting and piled up punishment that would begin to tell later on the older man. Gabe taking the punches and plodding after Sims steadily in spite of them, swinging hard and landing seldom. He connected with a few solid punches to the body that hurt Sims, but he couldn't tag him anywhere around the head.

Close to the end of the first round it looked for a moment as though the fight wasn't going to get much older. Sims saw an opening and brought a right upper-cut up from his belt that crashed into Gabe's chin and hurled him backward against the ropes. Sims leaped in and tried to finish it with lefts and rights that packed all his strength behind them. But Gabe managed to clinch, and hung on till the bell.

In the second round Sims gave up trying to end it in a hurry. Weaving and bobbing in and out, slipping most of Gabe's heavy swings, Sims concentrated on jabbing Gabe's eyes. By the end of the round, he had one o Gabe's eyes puffed shut and was starting to work on the other eye. At the bell, Rocky Gabe walked back to his corner and sat down like a man who'd already done more than a full day's labor.

At the start of the third round, Sims came out and went back instantly to jabbing lefts at Gabe's eyes. Gabe, gun-shy about his eyes by then, began jerking up his guard to protect them. And each time he did, Sims crossed a right to his body.

I began to think I was wrong. And if I was wrong about the fight, everything else I thought I'd figured out was wrong, too.

But then I noticed something. Sims's punches, which had been unerringly hitting their targets till then, were becoming less accurate. Some of them were going wild.

And then Gabe hit him. He just brought over a hay-maker right from behind his shoulder, the way he'd been doing from the start. But this time it landed. It slammed into the side of Sims's face and spun him completely around like a top.

A look of surprise came over Rocky Gabe's bruised and puffed face. But his ring instinct was quicker than his brain. He leaped in while Sims was still off balance and slugged Sims with a left to the ear and a right to the midsection.

Sims went backwards off his feet and sat down hard on the canvas.

The crowd, which had been pretty apathetic till then, came out of its seats with a scream of excitement.

Sims was back up on his feet by the count of two, apparently unhurt and still clearheaded. And for the rest of that round he managed to dodge and dance and side-step, avoiding getting tagged that solidly again.

But from the start of the fourth round, it was obvi-ous that the tide was beginning to turn. The timing of Sims's punches was off, just a little. He began to miss with swings more often than he landed. His footwork was getting sluggish and he was recovering too slowly from his swings, leaving himself open for precious split-seconds. And more of Gabe's roundhouses were connecting, doing damage.

Frankie Sims looked puzzled. In desperation, he be-gan trying to land the big one on Rocky Gabe's jaw, summoning everything he had behind his punches, leaving himself unguarded to do so. But there wasn't enough steam left in those punches to bother Gabe much. The fourth round was almost over when Gabe

took one of those punches in the face, deliberately step-
ping into it to clobber Sims with an overhanded right
that thudded off the side of Sims's jaw.

Sims's legs buckled under him. He sprawled face
down Gabe's feet.

Sims took a count of three before he started forcing
himself up on his knees. He was staggering to his feet
at the count of eight, his movements as uncoordinated
as a puppet's, when the bell sounded the end of the
round.

I slipped out of my seat and hurried down the aisle
to Bob Sherman, bent over to whisper in his ear: "Get
the Doc to check Sims. He's been doped."

Sherman jerked his head around to look up at me,
shocked. "What?"

"Doped," I told him. "In his water bottle, I'd
guess."

Sherman started to raise up out of his seat, then
hesitated, looking a little scared. "Wait a minute. You
sure? This could . . ."

"I'm *sure*," I told him flatly, and strode away
quickly up the aisle.

I'd left my Chevy parked a block from the Garden.
I was almost running when I reached it. I snapped on
the car radio as I pulled away from the curb and
headed for Van Eyck's hotel, tuned it in to the station
carrying the fight broadcast.

The news I wanted to hear wasn't long in coming.
The fight had been stopped. The sports announcer's
excited voice told listeners to hang on and wait for a
further announcement.

By the time I reached Van Eyck's hotel, the announcer was breathlessly spilling what had happened.
Frankie Sims's water bottle had been heavily laced with
sedative drugs. Both Steve Canby and Doug McAfee
denied knowing who put the drugs in the water. There
were no charges being placed against either of them

yet. But they were being held pending further investigation. Which suited me fine; it meant that Canby couldn't run.

The fight was declared void. Which meant that all bets were off. Exactly what I'd wanted.

I'd been right. Everything that had happened hung on that fight and the money to be made betting on it. With no bets being paid off, the whole setup would explode wide open and expose itself.

I parked in front of the hotel and went across the pavement and into the lobby, fast. I took the elevator up, strode through the corridor to Van Eyck's door and knocked.

I figured Van Eyck would be packing, getting set to blow town in a hurry. Because now he couldn't pay off Gus Banta tonight. And when he didn't show up with the dough, Banta's hoods would be coming after him.

I was only wrong about one thing. Banta's hoods weren't coming after Van Eyck. They'd been there with him, all the time.

It hit me when the door opened and I saw Benny standing there just inside the room, the .45 automatic in his small hand leveled at my guts.

I started to grab for my gun, stopped myself just in time. Remembering how I'd slugged him out with that gun, I knew he'd welcome any excuse to blow a hole through my middle.

"Well, well," he whispered happily. "Join us."

He backed away as I stepped inside at the summons of his gun. The huge hunk of beef called Buff stood against the wall to my left by the door, the mate to Benny's .45 in his massive fist. He kicked the door shut and took the .38 from my shoulder holster.

"Just like before, huh," Buff said, and laughed.

Van Eyck sat slumped on the edge of the bed, his bandaged and splinted left hand lying on his knee. He looked the way most men look when they know for certain that they are about to die.

Lavinia sat where I'd last seen her, as though she hadn't moved in all that time: in the chair by the window, staring out across the air shaft at the brick wall, trying to look like she believed that none of this concerned her at all.

A small radio lay smashed on the floor beside a lamp table.

Benny grinned when he saw me looking at it. "Some mess. We were all just sitting around here, listening to the fight. Henry here lost his head when he heard the news. Lousy, huh?"

I said, "I thought Banta didn't know where Van Eyck was getting the dough to pay him off."

"He didn't. Your visit made him curious. So he made Henry tell him. And we waited here with him to make sure. We were just about to leave. Now we can take you along, too. Gus'll be real glad to see you. You were gonna be our next job, anyway. Gus told you you'd regret pushing him around."

"I'm always regretting one thing or another," I said slowly.

"Sure. Like slugging me," Benny said and suddenly whipped up his arm and clouted the side of my skull with his .45.

Skyrockets burst inside my brain as I fell against the wall and slid down to the floor on my hands and knees. I stayed that way with my head hanging and the room dissolving in black mist around me and my scrambled brains urging me to get back up and fight; if I could just manage to last out that round, I could lick Rocky Gabe yet. The crowd was roaring for blood, but I couldn't get up.

And somewhere a voice that seemed to be coming through a distant loudspeaker was saying: "We'll take 'em down the back way, through the fire escape stairway. If anybody spots us, we'll say Barrow's passed out drunk. Can you carry him okay?"

Another voice said: "Easy."

"Okay, and I'll take care of Henry and the girl."

Something whipped through the air again and connected with the back of my head. It made something go click inside my skull. The fight was over. I couldn't even hear the referee counting me out.

TWENTY

"Hope I didn't hurt you, dear," a voice said. A hand slapped me, first one side of the face, then the other.

I forced my eyelids open. The voice and the slaps came from Benny. He was leaning over me. I saw his face first and then the .45 in his right hand. Instantly, he backed off to a safe distance. "Barrow's with us again," he announced.

"Good," Gus Banta said, nastily. "I want him to know what he's getting, when he gets it."

The back of my neck was as stiff as if my spinal cord had frozen together there. My head felt like it had been through a meat-grinder, inside and out. My mouth tasted of ashes and my hopes were lower than the floor I lay on.

I raised myself up to a sitting position with difficulty, leaning my back against the wall. Raising my groggy head, I looked around. We were in Gus Banta's office on the top of the parking garage. The door was shut, and Buff stood near it with his .45 ready. Van Eyck stood beside the table with the liquor bottles and glasses on it, leaning against the wall and staring at a spot on the opposite wall up near the ceiling. He looked like the thinnest of threads was holding him upright. Worse than frightened; he was beyond fright, in some limbo waiting to be dead.

Gus Banta sat behind his desk, watching me with those iceberg eyes of his, his bloated face a mask of sick evil.

Lavinia stood before his desk, trying to explain to him something that her look of hysteria made it obvious that she herself didn't believe.

"I don't belong in this!" she pleaded with him. "I told those two not to bring me here! I told you didn't want me. I'm no part of this!"

"You shouldn't've made that phone call to me that night," I told her. My voice sounded full of broken glass. "That put you in it."

She whirled to look at me. "I didn't know what that was all about! I still don't. Henry told me to do it. A gag, like. I swear I don't know . . ." She whirled back to face Banta. "Is that why I'm here? Because I don't know anything about any of this. Henry never told . . ."

"Shut your mouth," Banta told her without taking his eyes from me.

He got up from his chair and came around his desk and gazed down at me, smiling a little. "*You*," he whispered, "are gonna get it in the belly. So you'll linger and feel it for a while."

I tried to gather myself for a last big effort. It wouldn't save me. But I wanted to get my hands around Banta's thick neck before I was killed. It was no use, though. Parts of my brain were still out to lunch. My arms and legs wouldn't respond right to my commands. I knew I'd fumble it.

Still I had to try. I sat there motionless on the floor and worked desperately at bringing the different parts of me in contact with each other in time.

Gus Banta turned away and went to Van Eyck. "It's just business with you, Henry," he told the tall, thin gambler. "You can't pay. But you can still serve as a lesson to other guys thinking of welching. But we'll give it to you easy, in the head."

Van Eyck didn't respond. He might not have heard.

"We'll do it here," Banta said. "Sound won't carry far out've here. Put the three of them in the truck after and . . ."

"Why?" Lavinia pleaded, hysterically. "Why *me?* I never did anything to anybody!"

Banta shrugged. "Too bad. But you're a witness."

"I'm not! I swear I'll never tell anybody about this. I . . ."

Banta shook his head. "You're all out of luck, kid."

Lavinia cowered back against the desk, her exquisite face ugly with horror. She backed away around the desk to the wall behind it.

Buff took a few steps across the room toward her, his .45 ready. He said, "Keep away from that window, doll."

Lavinia pressed herself against the wall behind her as though she were trying to back clear through it and out of there.

I knew how she felt. I looked at the bottles of liquor on the table beside Van Eyck.

"Can I have a last drink?" I asked in my cracked voice.

Banta shook his head, turning away from Van Eyck to look at me wisely. "No, Barrow. And no chance to heave a bottle, either. You ran out of chances when you laid a hand on me." He looked at Buff and Benny. "All right. Let's get it . . ."

Lavinia suddenly unplastered herself from the wall, snatched the sharp-bladed letter opener from the top of Banta's desk.

Buff, who'd started to turn to finish Van Eyck, saw it first. He swung around fast for a shot at her. Lavinia threw her weapon before he could bring the gun to bear on her. Her aim justified her boast about her knife-throwing nightclub act. The letter opener flashed across the intervening space to Buff, the blade plunging deep into the center of his enormously wide chest. The .45 spilled out of his hand. He fell to his knees with a crash that shook the room, clutching awkwardly at the hilt of the thing protruding from his body. A gurgling scream of fear bubbled from his mouth.

Gus and Benny had already whirled toward Lavinia.

Benny's gun roared, the bullet hitting her high in the shoulder and dropping her behind the desk.

Buff's gun had skidded halfway across the room toward me. I made the supreme effort I'd been building to, shoving away from the wall and scrambling on my hands and knees for the fallen .45 in the same moment that Van Eyck abruptly came to life. He grabbed a quart whiskey bottle off the table beside him and smashed it to splinters against the back of Gus Banta's head.

It was Van Eyck's farewell gesture to life. As Banta fell, Benny spun and shot Van Eyck's face apart with a heavy .45 slug at close range.

I got both hands on Buff's .45, tried to balance myself on my shaky knees as I brought it up.

Benny whirled to face me, with his gun aimed at my face.

I fired first. I squeezed the trigger, felt the big gun buck in my hands as the cartridge exploded, watched the lead slug thud into Benny's chest and kick his whole body back against the wall.

His face died first. For a moment he stayed the way he was, as though the bullet had pinned him to the wall. Then he began sliding down it.

But the gun in his hand roared one last time before he went all the way down.

I felt a shock of pain rip across the top of my skull as the slug creased my scalp. The .45 went out of my hands as I was knocked backwards to the floor.

I rolled quickly, instinctively fearing another shot from him. None came. Straining to hang onto consciousness just a little longer, I dragged myself off the floor on my hands and knees.

Someone else was still moving in the room. I forced my head around and looked toward Benny. He lay motionless against the wall. There was another sound: a harsh, dragging cry of pain. I looked toward it.

Buff was up on his knees across the room, swaying, pulling the letter opener slowly out of his chest.

The sound I'd heard was coming out of his wide-open mouth. His eyes were glazing with encroaching death. But still he pulled at the hilt. I stared, watching the blade emerge from him, little by little. Finally he got it all the way out, his blood dripping from the blade.

He shoved himself slowly around on his knees, the monstrous bulk of his torso sagging, his glazed eyes searching—till they fastened on me.

We stared at each other across the room. Then, the long blade protruding out from his fist, he started slowly, painfully, dragging himself toward me on his knees.

I looked around desperately for the .45 but a dark reddish fog seemed to be rising up from the floor all around me. I couldn't see the gun so I tried to find it by blindly plunging my hands into the fog and groping around for it. I still couldn't find it.

I began desperately crawling away from him. He crawled after me, the letter opener in his huge fist, blood pumping out of the wound in his massive chest. We both could move only slowly, with great effort. We were both in pain, both dazed and struggling to stay conscious. Buff's pursuit of me became a hideous slow motion nightmare with Buff crawling slowly after me, trying to get at me with that long sharp blade; and me crawling slowly away from him, working my way around chairs, the desk. The outcome depended on which of us could hang on to consciousness longer.

I crawled over something. Lavinia's legs. They moved at my touch.

Bumped against something else. A man's body in the fog obscuring the floor. He didn't move. I worked my way around him.

Felt something stinging my knees, hurting them. I bent awkwardly, felt around with my hands. Realized I was touching pieces of broken glass.

I turned my head and looked behind me. Buff was getting nearer. The blade in his grasp looked longer, deadlier.

I fumbled around on the floor with my outstretched hands, desperate in my search. And at last I found it.

I straightened on my knees, turned to face the dying mammoth who was pursuing me with my death in his hand. I brought up what I had found: the neck of the bottle Van Eyck had used to cave in Gus Banta's skull. I gripped it tightly in my right hand, the jagged glass ends pointed out at Buff.

The sight of this new weapon stopped him. Slowly, he raised his eyes from it to my face. We stayed that way, on our knees, staring at each other, not moving except for our labored breathing. Each with a weapon ready. Each waiting for the other to make a move or go down.

And then, watching him and waiting, I saw him stop breathing. His chest wasn't heaving, and no sound came from his open mouth. Abruptly as that, he was dead. I watched his glazed eyes go utterly empty, watched him settle in a bulky mound face down on the floor.

I dropped the neck of the bottle and dragged myself to the desk. Reaching up, I felt across the top of it till I found the telephone, clawed it off. It fell with a crash to the floor beside me. I felt the dial with my fingers till I found the last dial hole, O for operator, and spun it with a trembling forefinger. I fumbled and managed to lift the receiver to my mouth and told the operator it was an emergency. I asked for Lieutenant Sellers of

。

Homicide, in a hurry. I had to tell her twice before she understood me. I was fighting surging waves of dizziness with the last frail fringes of will power when Sellers' voice came through the receiver. The voice in which I managed to tell him where to find me sounded a long way off. I tried telling him more:

"It was Steve Canby," I rasped. "There was a picture. Lewis . . ."

But then whatever had been holding me up snapped.

I let go of the phone. The red mist rising from the floor rose higher, engulfing me, and I sank into its bottomless depths.

TWENTY-ONE

It was two days before the doctors at Bellevue Hospital let me all the way up out of sedation. My head was going to be all right; there was nothing fractured. But two concussions in a row had done a shock job on my nervous system, and absolute rest was in order to make sure I got back to normal. I had no complaints; I was glad to be alive. The only other one who'd come out of Banta's office alive was Lavinia. She was in another room on the same floor, recovering from the removal of the bullet from her shoulder.

Lieutenant Sellers was the first visitor they allowed me. He sat on the chair beside my bed, looking his usual weary self.

"I hear you've been yelling for me all the time in your sleep," he said. "I didn't know you cared."

"I had to tell you, there's a picture—a photograph—Ernest Lewis took. You've got to find it. It's . . ."

Sellers nodded. "I know. We found it. On Van Eyck's body."

He took a four-by-five photograph from his pocket

and showed it to me. "This is a copy of it. We faced Canby with it yesterday. He broke down and spilled his guts for us."

I looked at the picture. It showed the bedroom of Angela Hart's luxury suite. In the center of the photo was Steve Canby, a look of rage twisting his face and a large wrought-iron ashtray in his hand. He was standing over a man who lay sprawled face down on the carpet.

I touched a finger to the man lying at Canby s feet. "Roland Miller."

Sellers nodded, eyeing me with curiosity. "How'd you know about the picture?"

"There had to be one like it," I told him. "It fitted that way. The trick mirror in Angela Hart's bedroom closet. Her boy friend Lewis being a photographer. And Canby feeling the way he did about Angela. He was crazy for her. Even knowing she was a tramp, he had to have her. And he wanted her for himself, but he couldn't have her that way. There were too many other men. Canby tried to get her out of his system, but he couldn't. He tried to forget her after she made a play for Frankie Sims. Yet when he caught her later with Doug McAfee, he went nuts and attacked McAfee. And then he tried to forget her again. But it was no good. It was a sickness with him, I guess. And the sickness got worse when he couldn't have her, when she was with her other boy friends."

"Right so far," Sellers said. "He told us he began following her, even after she took up with Roland Miller and didn't come to him at all anymore."

"The way I figured it," I told him, "Canby finally couldn't stand it. So he busted in on Miller and Angela in the love-nest Miller set her up in. He lost his head and killed Miller."

"Canby claims it was sort of self-defense. He says when he walked in on them, Roland Miller got furious and started slugging him. Miller was a much bigger man. And by then Canby was all twisted up inside with rage and jealousy and frustration, anyway. So he picked up that heavy iron ashtray and hit Miller with it. Claims he was so worked up he stood like he is in that picture for a long time, before he realized he'd killed a man. I guess his lawyer'll try getting him off on an insanity plea. He says he didn't know what he was doing."

"He'll play hell trying to make that stick for the other murders," I said.

Lieutenant Sellers sighed. "I don't know. When you get these complicated ones in front of juries . . . All I know is, it's a lucky break we've got this picture as evidence. I'm still not quite sure how come there is a picture like this." He looked questioningly at me.

"Roland Miller liked variety. He'd had his fling with Angela, and he was getting ready to drop her for a new girl he'd just hired. Angela knew that. Maybe she'd even been expecting it, knowing the way he was. And she liked the life Miller was giving her. She wanted to hold onto the things big money like he had could buy her."

I tapped the photo. "So Angela and another of her playmates, Ernest Lewis, got a great idea. A trick mirror and a hole cut in the bedroom closet door behind it. The idea was for Lewis to hide in the closet and shoot pictures of Angela and Miller in bed together. Miller'd pay a lot for those pictures. If they got to his wife, he'd have to shell out even more in alimony. His wife didn't give a damn about Miller, except for his dough. There may have been more pictures. Maybe Lewis was shooting a lot of them, on different nights, to make sure they had Miller cold. Anyway, Lewis was in the closet with his camera ready when Canby stormed in on Miller and Angela. And he got this picture of Canby standing over the man he'd killed, with the murder weapon in his hand. So the blackmail idea could still work for Lewis and Angela. Only the victim was Canby, instead of Miller."

Sellers took the photograph back from me and slipped it in his pocket. "Canby says he collapsed in a crying fit when he realized what he'd done. When he finally got hold of himself, there was Lewis and Angela standing over him, ready with a proposition to help him cover up the killing, for a price. He was nuts to go through with it. If he'd called us right away, he'd have gotten away with a self-defense plea, plus a dose of temporary insanity, with a smart lawyer. But he was too stunned right then to think straight. He was scared silly. So he agreed."

We went over the rest of it together, each of us filling in the separate details we knew.

They'd waited in Angela's apartment till the late dark hours of morning. Then Canby and Lewis had taken Miller's body out via the fire escape to Lewis' car, parked in back of the building. They drove to another part of town and dumped Miller's body in an alley, after taking all the money Miller had on him to make it look like a robbery mugging.

After that, Angela and Lewis, with the photograph as their weapon, blackmailed Steve Canby relentlessly. He paid and paid . . . till it hurt.

And then Van Eyck came along, desperate for money, trying to arrange for Frankie Sims to take a dive. Canby got mad at the time and tossed Van Eyck out. But later he'd begun thinking about all the tough, slimy characters a guy like Van Eyck knew. And he began to feel a kind of kindredship with Van Eyck. They were both of them desperate men, with their lives at stake.

So the two of them got together and worked out a deal conceived out of their mutual desperation: Van Eyck would get the photo and get rid of Angela and Lewis in such a way that Canby couldn't be connected

with it. Canby in payment would see to it that Frankie
Sims lost the fight, Van Eyck would win enough money
to pay off his debt and get off Banta's deadly hook.
Canby would get out from under the twin horns of
blackmail and a murder rap.

Afterwards, Van Eyck would have the photo as a
guarantee that Canby lived up to his part of the bargain. And neither one of them could spill on the other
without implicating himself.

The night it was planned for had started exactly as
planned. Canby made a point of being seen having a
gay time at the Oran Club and later at the party he
took the dancer to. That was the point of Van Eyck
handling the murders: He had no past connections
with Angela or Lewis, to tie him in any way with their
deaths.

Van Eyck and the two killers he'd hired with
Canby's money went to Ernest Lewis' apartment. They
beat him till he showed them where he'd hidden the
blackmail photo. Then they killed him. So far, as
planned. But then complications began to crop up.

The first complication was Nel Tarey. She was
Lewis' secretary; there was no knowing if she was
aware of the blackmail setup, and they were taking no
chances. They went to her apartment to rub her out,
but she wasn't there. Luckily for her, she was waiting
out a late flight with a friend at Idlewild Airport that
entire night.

The next complication was that they didn't finish
off Angela Hart that night. Mainly because of the third
complication that showed up: Me.

Angela Hart had come into the Oran Club looking
for Canby. She'd found Lewis dead in his apartment
and knew she was next on the list. She hadn't figured
that their little blackmail scheme would get that rough.
So she'd gone looking for Canby, probably to try talking him into forgetting the whole thing. Hoping she
could persuade him to let her live in exchange for her

dropping the blackmail and swearing never to mention it to anyone. It was a pretty slim possibility, but about all that was left to her. Unless she wanted to go to the police for protection and in doing so set herself up for a charge of blackmail and withholding knowledge of a murder.

She didn't find Canby that night. But she did run into me. Once I entered the picture, everything began going wrong with the plans of Canby and Van Eyck. Culminating in the night of the fight, when I tipped off the doping of Frankie Sims. . . .

It was three days later when I left the hospital. I dropped into Lavinia's room to say goodbye before leaving. She was recovering rapidly and had convinced the cops that she hadn't known what it was all about when Van Eyck persuaded her to decoy me out of my apartment with that phoney phone call. Which was all right with me, whether it was true or not.

She told me, "Thanks for backing me up on my story with the cops, Jake. I appreciate it. I guess you had to lie a little."

"You earned it," I said. "If you hadn't tossed that letter opener when you did, we'd both have been meals for a lot of fish by now."

She looked pleased. "Yeah. I was pretty good in there, wasn't I? I'm going back to the knife act when I get out of here." She quirked a grin at me. "Care to join me, as my partner in the act?"

"No, thanks. I've already seen a demonstration of what could happen if you got sore at me."

We laughed and shook hands on that and I promised to drop in to see her again during visiting hours.

Fred Usher's check for two thousand dollars was waiting for me at my apartment. I was having a drink and admiring the numbers on the check when Nel

Tarey showed up.

We settled on the sofa and had a few drinks together, and after a while she said, "What you need is a secretary, Jake. And I happen to be a secretary who's out of a job."

"What is this, a job application?"

"Uh-huh. Sort of."

"I can't afford a secretary," I told her.

"You can now. The two thousand dollars."

"I'm using that for a vacation. Doctor's orders."

"But you'll be back."

"By then I won't be able to afford you again."

"Are you sure?" she murmured, moving closer to me. "I'm quite an exceptional secretary. Very talented."

"How about a demonstration?" I suggested and kissed her luscious mouth.

She demonstrated. When we came up for air, I nodded. "Very talented," I agreed. "Would you consider a little part-time evening work?"

She rubbed her cheek against my shoulder, like a kitten. "Hmmmm. Maybe. If the inducement were strong enough."

"I try my best," I told her. "How're you at taking dictation?"

"It's my best feature," she whispered, and nibbled at my earlobe. "Taking dictation."

"On the boss's lap?"

"Especially that way." She wriggled onto my lap. "All right, sir," she said, with a proper, businesslike expression, "go ahead and dictate."

I started to.

The job application demonstration, as it developed, continued on into the night. And she'd told the truth. She was very, very good at taking dictation.

THE END

Marvin H. Albert was born January 22, 1924 in Philadelphia, Pennsylvania, and served as a radio officer in the Merchant Marine during World War II. After working as the director of a children's  theater troupe in Philadelphia, he moved to New York in 1950 and began writing and editing for the magazines *Quick and Look*. Albert turned to writing full time after the success of his novel *The Law and Jake Wade* in 1956. He wrote under a variety of pseudonyms in a variety of genres, including mysteries, westerns and movie novelizations. In 1965 he moved to Los Angeles, where he began writing screenplays, then moved to the south of France in 1976. That year, the Mystery Writers of America named his thriller, *Gargoyle Conspiracy,* the best mystery of the year. Albert died of a heart attack on March 24, 1996, in Menton, France.

Marvin H. Albert Bibliography
(1924-1996)

Crime/Adventure

As by Marvin Albert (Pete Sawyer series):
The Dark Goddess (Doubleday, 1978; Dell, 1979)
Stone Angel (Fawcett Gold Medal, 1986)
Back in the Real World (Fawcett Gold Medal, 1986)
Get Off at Babylon (Fawcett Gold Medal, 1987)
Long Teeth (Fawcett Gold Medal, 1987)
The Last Smile (Fawcett Gold Medal, 1988)
The Midnight Sister (Fawcett Gold Medal, 1989)
Bimbo Heaven (Fawcett Gold Medal, 1990)
The Zig-Zag Man (Fawcett Gold Medal, 1991)
The Riviera Contract (Fawcett Gold Medal, 1992)

As by Marvin H. Albert:
Lie Down with Lions (Gold Medal, 1959)
The Gargoyle Conspiracy (Doubleday, 1975; Dell, 1982)
Hidden Lives (Delacorte, 1981; Dell, 1982)
The Medusa Complex (Arbor House, 1982; Zebra, 1983)
Operation Lila (Arbor House, 1983; Zebra, 1985)
The Golden Circle (Beach Books/National Press, 1987; no paperback)

As by J. D. Christilian:
Scarlet Women (Donald I. Fine, 1996; Signet 1997)

As by Al Conroy (Soldato series)
#1. Soldato! (Lancer, 1972)
#2. Death Grip! (Lancer, 1972)
#3. Strangle Hold! (Lancer, 1973; ghost-written by Gil Brewer)

#4. Murder Mission! (Lancer, 1973)
#5. Blood Run! (Lancer, 1973; ghost-written by Gil
    Brewer)

As by Albert Conroy:
The Road's End (Gold Medal, 1952)
The Chiselers (Gold Medal, 1953)
Nice Guys Finish Dead (Gold Medal, 1957)
The Mob Says Murder (Gold Medal, 1958)
Murder in Room 13 (Gold Medal, 1958)
Devil in Dungarees (Crest, 1960)
Mr. Lucky (Dell, 1960; TV tie-in)
The Looters (Crest, 1961)

As by Ian MacAlister (adventure series):
Skylark Mission (Gold Medal, 1973)
Driscoll's Diamonds (Gold Medal, 1973)
Strike Force 7 (Gold Medal, 1974)
Valley of the Assassins (Gold Medal, 1976)

As by Nick Quarry (Jake Barrow series):
The Hoods Come Calling (Gold Medal, 1958)
Trail of a Tramp (Gold Medal, 1958)
The Girl with No Place to Hide (Gold Medal, 1959)
No Chance in Hell (Gold Medal, 1960)
Till It Hurts (Gold Medal, 1960)
Some Die Hard (Gold Medal, 1961)

Mafia:
The Don Is Dead (Gold Medal, 1972)
The Vendetta (Gold Medal, 1973)

As by Anthony Rome (Tony Rome series):
Miami Mayhem (Pocket Book, 1960; filmed as *Tony*

Rome, 1967)

The Lady in Cement (Pocket Book, 1961; filmed in 1968)

My Kind of Game (Dell, 1962)

[entire series reprinted as by Marvin Albert by Fawcett Gold Medal, 1988-89]

Westerns

As by Marvin Albert:

The Law and Jake Wade (Gold Medal, 1956)

Apache Uprising (Gold Medal, 1957; reprinted as *Duel at Diablo*, 1966, movie tie-in)

The Bounty Killer (Gold Medal, 1958; filmed as *The Ugly Ones*, 1966)

Renegade Posse (Gold Medal, 1958; filmed as *Bullet for a Bad Man*, 1964)

The Reformed Gun (Gold Medal, 1959)

Rider from Wind River (Gold Medal, 1959)

Posse at High Pass (Gold Medal, 1964)

As by Al Conroy (Clayburn series):

Clayburn (Dell, 1961)

Last Train to Bannock (Dell, 1963)

Three Rode North (Dell, 1964)

The Man in Black (Dell, 1965; filmed as *Rough Night in Jericho*, 1967)

[entire series reprinted as by Marvin Albert by Fawcett Gold Medal, 1989-90]

Movie Adaptations

As by Marvin Albert:

Party Girl (Gold Medal, 1958)

That Jane from Maine (Gold Medal, 1959; released as *It Happened to Jane*)

Pillow Talk (Gold Medal, 1959)
All the Young Men (Cardinal/Pocket, 1960)
Force of Impulse (Popular Library, 1960)
Come September (Dell, 1961)
Lover Come Back (Gold Medal, 1962)
Move Over, Darling (Dell, 1963)
Palm Springs Weekend (Dell, 1963)
Under the Yum Yum Tree (Dell, 1963)
The V.I.P.s (Dell, 1963)
Goodbye Charlie (Dell, 1964)
Honeymoon Hotel (Dell, 1964)
The Outrage (Pocket, 1964)
The Pink Panther (Bantam, 1964)
Do Not Disturb (Dell, 1965)
The Great Race (Dell, 1965)
Strange Bedfellows (Pyramid, 1965)
A Very Special Favor (Dell, 1965)
What's New Pussycat (Dell, 1965)
Crazy Joe (Bantam, 1974; as by Mike Barone)
The Untouchables (Ivy, 1987)

Screenplays

Duel at Diablo (1966, based on *Apache Uprising*)
Rough Night in Jericho (1967, based on *The Man in Black*)
Lady in Cement (1968, based on his novel of the same name)
A Twist of Sand (1968; based on the novel by Geoffrey Jenkins)
The Don Is Dead (1973, based on his novel of the same name)

Non-Fiction

Becoming a Mother: What Every Woman Ought to Know About Fertility, Conception, Pregnancy and Childbirth (David McKay, 1955; co-authored by Theodore R. Seidman)

Broadsides and Boarders (Appleton-Century-Crofts, 1957; history of sailing ships)

The Long White Road: Ernest Shackleton's Antarctic Adventures (David McKay, 1957; Pyramid, 1960)

The Divorce (Simon & Schuster, 1965; Henry VIII, his queen, and his mistress)

Black Gat Books

Black Gat Books is a new line of mass market paperbacks introduced in 2015 by Stark House Press. New titles appear every other month, featuring the best in crime fiction reprints. Each book is size to 4.25" x 7", just like they used to be, and priced at $9.99 (1–31) and $10.99 (32–). Collect them all.

1 Haven for the Damned
   by Harry Whittington
   978-1-933586-75-5

2 Eddie's World
   by Charlie Stella
   978-1-933586-76-2

3 Stranger at Home
   by Leigh Brackett
   writing as
   George Sanders
   978-1-933586-78-6

4 The Persian Cat
   by John Flagg
   978-1933586-90-8

5 Only the Wicked
   by Gary Phillips
   978-1-933586-93-9

6 Felony Tank
   by Malcolm Braly
   978-1-933586-91-5

7 The Girl on the Bestseller List
   by Vin Packer
   978-1-933586-98-4

8 She Got What She Wanted
   by Orrie Hitt
   978-1-944520-04-5

9 The Woman on the Roof
   by Helen Nielsen
   978-1-944520-13-7

10 Angel's Flight
   by Lou Cameron
   978-1-944520-18-2

11 The Affair of Lady Westcott's Lost Ruby /
   The Case of the Unseen Assassin by Gary Lovisi
   978-1-944520-22-9

12 The Last Notch
   by Arnold Hano
   978-1-944520-31-1

13 Never Say No to a Killer
   by Clifton Adams
   978-1-944520-36-6

14 The Men from the Boys
   by Ed Lacy
   978-1-944520-46-5

15 Frenzy of Evil
   by Henry Kane
   978-1-944520-53-3

16 You'll Get Yours
   by William Ard
   978-1-944520-54-0

17 End of the Line
   by Dolores &
   Bert Hitchens
   978-1-9445205-7

18 Frantic
   by Noël Calef
   978-1-944520-66-3

19 The Hoods Take Over
   by Ovid Demaris
   978-1-944520-73-1

20 Madball
   by Fredric Brown
   978-1-944520-74-8

21 Stool Pigeon
   by Louis Malley
   978-1-944520-81-6

22 The Living End
   by Frank Kane
   978-1-944520-81-6

23 My Old Man's Badge
   by Ferguson Findley
   978-1-9445208-78-3

24 Tears Are For Angels
   by Paul Connelly
   978-1-944520-92-2

25 Two Names for Death
   by E. P. Fenwick
   978-195147301-3

26 Dead Wrong
   by Lorenz Heller
   978-1951473-03-7

27 Little Sister
   by Robert Martin
   978-1951473-07-5

28 Satan Takes the Helm
   By Calvin Clements
   978-1-951473-14-3

29 Cut Me In
   by Jack Karney
   978-1-951473-18-1

30 Hoodlums
   by George Benet
   978-1-951473-23-5

31 So Young, So Wicked
   by Jonathan Craig
   978-1-951473-30-3

32 Tears of Jessie Hewett
   by Edna Sherry
   978-1-951473-36-5

33 Repeat Performance
   by William O'Farrell
   978-1-951473-42-6

Stark House Press

1315 H Street, Eureka, CA 95501 707-498-3135 griffinskye3@sbcglobal.net www.starkhousepress.com
Available from your local bookstore or direct from the publisher.

Made in the USA
Monee, IL
24 December 2021